I was born in Bucharest, and during the war I went to Palestine. That's World War II, in case you didn't know. My father was a Rumanian journalist who was always "off somewhere." That's what my mother used to tell me. When I was little, I thought he had two professions: journalism and being off somewhere. My mother stayed with me at home. I was a terror.

"In Lydia, Mr. Orlev has created a real hero, one that wins our admiration but never our pity. Children will love her, will cheer her on in her battles, and be uplifted by her triumphs. And they'll learn some fiendishly clever pranks along the way." —*New York Times Book Review*

"Often outrageous and abrasive, yet also delightfully imaginative and bright, Lydia is the very archetype of a survivor." —*Kirkus Reviews*, pointer review

"What we have here is a children's book set during the Holocaust where children are more important than history, more important even than the moral message we are intended to derive from history. . . . For every angry child who ever resisted the horrible fate of being good, Lydia is an inspiration, a role model, and most of all, a friend." —*Booklist*, starred review

OTHER PUFFIN BOOKS ABOUT WORLD WAR II

LYDIA,
Queen of Palestine

❧

URI ORLEV

Translated from the Hebrew by Hillel Halkin

PUFFIN BOOKS

PUFFIN BOOKS
Published by the Penguin Group
Penguin Books USA Inc., 375 Hudson Street, New York, New York 10014, U.S.A.
Penguin Books Ltd, 27 Wrights Lane, London W8 5TZ, England
Penguin Books Australia Ltd, Ringwood, Victoria, Australia
Penguin Books Canada Ltd, 10 Alcorn Avenue, Toronto, Ontario, Canada M4V 3B2
Penguin Books (N.Z.) Ltd, 182-190 Wairau Road, Auckland 10, New Zealand

Penguin Books Ltd, Registered Offices: Harmondsworth, Middlesex, England

First published in Israel as *Lidyah, malkat erets yisra 'el* by
Keter Publishing House, 1991

First published in the United States of America by Houghton Mifflin Company, 1993
Published in Puffin Books, 1995

1 3 5 7 9 10 8 6 4 2

LIBRARY OF CONGRESS CATALOGING-IN-PUBLICATION DATA
Orlev, Uri.
[Lidyah, malkat Erets Yisra 'el. English]
Lydia, Queen of Palestine / Uri Orlev; translated from the Hebrew by Hillel Halkin.   p.   cm.
Summary: Ten-year-old Lydia describes her childhood escapades in pre–World War II
Romania, her struggles to understand her parents' divorce
amid the chaos of the war, and her life on a kibbutz in Palestine.
Based on the life of the Israeli poet Arianna Haran.
ISBN 0-14-037089-7
[1. Jews—Romania—Fiction. 2. World War, 1939–1945—Jews—Romania—Fiction.
3. Divorce—Fiction. 4. Kibbutzim—Fiction. 5. Romania—Fiction. 6. Israel—Fiction.]
I. Halkin, Hillel.   II. Title.
PZ7.O6333Ly   1995   [Fic]—dc20   94-30188   CIP   AC

Printed in the United States of America

Contents

CHAPTER ONE

All About Me

I WAS BORN IN 1933 in Bucharest, Romania, and during
the war I went to Palestine. That's World War II, in
case you didn't know. My father was a Romanian journalist who was always "off somewhere." That's what my
mother used to tell me. When I was little, I thought he
had two professions: journalism and being off somewhere.
My mother stayed at home with me. I was a terror.

Every summer we went to the mountains. I used to
wait for this all year, because the farmer and his wife who
rented us a wing of their house had two sons, Ion and
Mihai. They were just as wild as I was, and there was no
one to watch us or keep tabs on us.

I was jealous of the two of them for having the mountains to live in all year long. Ion and Mihai taught me to
climb rocks, to cross streams on stones, to pee standing
up like a boy, and to go barefoot. Come to think of it,
I was already going barefoot before I knew them. My
mother had bought me a new pair of red-and-white san-

dals, and on our first day in the moutains, I went for a walk by a stream that ran near the house and stepped in some cow poop. I slipped my foot out of my sandal and came home wearing only one shoe. When my mother wanted to know where the other sandal was, I told her that I couldn't remember. I wasn't about to have her clean it off and make me wear it.

She lost her temper and said, "Do you have any idea what those sandals cost? Now you can go barefoot."

"Don't think that I won't," I said.

You see, I thought there was nothing I couldn't do.

I went out without shoes and everything jabbed my feet, but I kept on going. Ion and Mihai walked behind me, snickering.

"Keeping your good shoes for church?" Mihai asked.

"Don't be a dope," said Ion. "Don't you know city folk never take their shoes off? They even sleep in them."

"They do not," I said. "And you've got no right to laugh, because you have calluses on your feet and I don't. That's because I'm a princess."

I wasn't making that up. I had heard the farmer's wife telling an old peasant woman that "the girl staying in our house goes about dressed like a princess."

They looked at my feet and saw I was right. "You can't marry Prince Michael," I told them, "if you don't have silky skin on your feet."

Prince Michael, in case you didn't know, was the son of the King of Romania. Maybe my friend Mihai was named after him. All this was before I decided to go with Prince Michael to Palestine.

They must have believed me, because they believed in magic and thought I was special. So did I. I told them that I only washed my hair with pure rainwater from a barrel.

"For someone so special," said Ion, "you're pretty dumb. All the women in the village wash their hair with rainwater, and they're nothing but a bunch of peasants."

"But look at their feet!"

They couldn't argue with that.

Examining each other's feet made us friends. I used to rush through breakfast every morning just to see them, which wasn't easy, because I loved to eat. Usually they were already waiting for me on the steps, grinning quietly. They weren't generally so quiet, but they behaved themselves near my mother because they were afraid of her. She didn't allow them to shout or whistle for me in the morning. They weren't afraid of their own mother, although she was stronger than mine. They were good and scared of their father, though.

Ion and Mihai were afraid of my mother because they had heard a woman whisper to the grocer that she was "a city witch." And they were afraid of their father because anyone would have been.

"Just you wait until your Pa comes home," their mother used to threaten them.

That first summer we were caught pinning together two women in the grocery. We did it with safety pins, and when one of them turned to go, she ripped her skirt. Ion and Mihai's father found out about it that evening. From their room we could hear their mother telling him.

3

I asked them what he would do and they said, "He'll tan our hides with a belt. Doesn't yours?"

They didn't believe me when I told them that he didn't. I was about to go upstairs to my room when their father walked in and asked me, "Just where do you think you're going?"

"You can't do anything to me," I told him. "You're not my father."

"That's so," he said. "Your punishment will be to watch."

He yanked the belt out of his pants with a single motion that sent it whistling through the air. You could have passed out just from that. Mihai went first. He was pale and shaking all over, but he didn't cry or call for his mother or try to run away. He knew it was no use. He lay across his father's knee and got whacked only once, but real hard. That's when he began whimpering "Ma!" He wasn't even calling for help then; he just said it because it hurt. Then it was Ion's turn. He got three whacks, because he was bigger and supposed to be more responsible. Ion cried, too, but not so loud. To teach me a lesson, his father made him turn around and pull down his pants. There were three red welts on his behind. His father thought it would embarrass him to have to strip in front of me. He didn't know that we skinny-dipped together in the stream.

The welts didn't seem like a big deal to me. Once my mother had gotten mad and spanked me too; it left a red handprint on my bottom that made her feel sorry by just looking at it. I didn't tell Ion and Mihai about it, though, because mothers weren't supposed to hit you. To tell the

4

truth, those welts scared me less than that belt whipping out of those pants.

I'm not sure if it was that summer or the next one when we were caught slicking the plank bridging the stream with my mother's soap. First, though, we watched one of the neighbors lose her balance and fall into the water. Her husband came, sniffed the plank, realized that the soap wasn't local, and told my mother, who discovered that a bar of her soap was missing. When Ion and Mihai's father came home that evening, he asked them if we had done it. Since he warned them that they would catch it twice as bad if they lied, they told the truth. Once they had confessed, I did, too.

Their father reached for his belt. I felt sick. Out it came — and down went his pants. He managed to grab them at the last moment. The three of us tried keeping a straight face, but it was more funny than scary. Mihai was the first to start laughing, and Ion and I joined him. We couldn't stop. Their father gave us a furious look and suddenly burst out laughing, too. He was whooping so hard that his wife came running in a fright and my mother hurried downstairs. In the end, he let us off. I say "us," because having to watch my friends get whipped really was a punishment for me.

There was only one day a week when they never fooled around, or rather, half a day. Every Sunday their mother dressed them in their best clothes, which they weren't allowed to get dirty. She and her husband put on their Sunday best, too, and all four of them went off to church. My mother and I stayed behind. They thought that was because we were city folk, and I did, too. Ion and Mihai were a sorry sight in their good clothes. Although this amounted to nothing more than a white shirt and clean pants, they thought it cost a lot of money, because that's what they were told at home. And maybe it really was a lot for their parents. They had to wear shoes, too, which were polished until they gleamed. They weren't allowed to take them off until church was out. Mihai wore Ion's old shoes, which were big on him, and for a while Ion hobbled to church and back in shoes that were too small. His mother had promised to buy him a new pair in a year, but meanwhile his feet kept growing and he had to borrow an old pair of his father's. I never told him, but despite all that shoe polish he looked like Charlie Chaplin in them. Not that he seemed to mind. Lots of boys in the village went about in their father's old things.

When the weather was nice, we went to the stream, took off our clothes, and jumped in. I remember the first time they saw my panties. They had never seen anything like them before. And I had never seen a naked boy.

They had a feud with someone in the village, a man who once stole a pig of theirs and refused to own up. Maybe he had confessed to the priest, but the priest wasn't allowed to tell on him. The man said the pig belonged to him and he slaughtered it. Ion and Mihai's mother even fought with his wife in the grocery and pulled her hair.

The two boys explained to me that this man, his wife, and their dog were "official enemies," but that their daughters were not, because girls — especially little ones — didn't count. Since this hurt my feelings, they said that city girls were different. Once you were an official enemy, anything could be done to you. You could even be killed. I found that hard to believe. But of course, all this was before the war.

Sometimes we snuck into the enemy's sheep pen, opened the gate, and let out all his sheep. Or else we threw stones at his dog. Or shoplifted from his wife's store. Ion and Mihai would buy some small item to keep her busy, because they knew they could never get away with it themselves. The woman watched them like a hawk, but she never suspected me, the city girl who dressed like a princess.

When it rained, we took cover in the barn and played house in the hayloft. Mihai was always the baby. We would send him down below and tell him we would call him when it was time for him to be born. It made him mad to wait, and in the end, there was sure to be a fight that I would have to break up. After that we played doctor. Sometimes I was the patient and sometimes I was the doctor. At first the boys didn't believe that girls could be doctors, but I told them to ask my father.

My father came on weekends and then we went for long walks, because that was something he liked to do.

My name was Lydia. It still is, because when I came to Palestine I refused to change it to a Hebrew name. My mother was short and pretty — or at least, I thought she was. My father was handsome and very tall. I was always the tallest and strongest girl in my class. And the prettiest. We lived in Bucharest. That's the capital of Romania, in case you didn't know. Our neighbors weren't Jewish, but they were all rich, and I didn't know I was different until the war broke out. We just didn't celebrate the same holidays that they did, except for birthdays. And once, before I knew I was Jewish, I remember being told by my mother that she wasn't going to cook that day.

"You'll eat out with your father," she said.

"What about you?"

"I'm not eating today. I'm fasting."

"How come? Don't you feel well?"

"I feel fine. But today is a special day that I fast on."

I burst into tears and tugged at her dress, because the "special day" scared me. In the end she had to agree to come with us to the restaurant. I don't remember if she ate anything there, but she never mentioned the "special day" again.

I found out that we were Jewish by accident. We had a neighbor who was an Eastern Orthodox priest and I used to play with his children. One day I asked if I could go to church with them. He said, "Of course, but you'll have to ask your mother for permission. If she agrees, you're welcome to come."

I ran to ask her. She laughed and asked, "Why on earth would you want to go to church? We're Jewish."

"What's that?"

"The Jews are a very old people, and we belong to it."

"Papa too?"

"Papa too. Our whole family."

"You mean we're not Romanians?"

"We're Romanians because we're citizens of Romania, but we're also Jews."

"You mean we're like Gypsies?"

"Gypsies? What an idea! Gypsies are Gypsies and Jews are Jews. The two have nothing in common."

I asked if we were like the Jews in Dudeşti, which was a Jewish slum in Bucharest. My mother wasn't thrilled by this comparison either. The Jews there were Jews too, she said, but not all Jews were the same.

"Some day you'll understand."

There were lots of things that I was supposed to understand some day.

"We Jews are a very ancient people that is scattered all over, because we were exiled from our land. We've given the world many great men. Even Jesus was a Jew."

"When were we exiled?"

"Two thousand years ago. Do you have any idea how long ago that is?"

"I'll bet Grandma wasn't even born then."

My mother laughed. She said it was much longer ago than that, before my grandmother's grandmother's grandmother was born. I didn't know whether to believe her or not, so I told her not to exaggerate. It always annoyed her when I asked her something and then started to argue about it. It made her stop in the middle. I had to beg her to go on.

"All right, Mama, I promise to listen and not argue."

"We're in exile, but we still have a homeland. You can't say that about the Gypsies."

"How can we have a home we never lived in?"

"We may not have lived in it, but our ancestors did."

"Where is it?"

9

"In Palestine."

"Is that why we shout, 'Kikes, go to Palestine'?"

My mother was shocked. "*You* shout 'Kikes, go to Palestine'?"

Now it was my turn to be alarmed. "I only did it once, Mama. Everyone did."

"All right. Now you know better. I've told you a thousand times not to play with that riffraff. And I want you to know that the Jews in Palestine are free and proud."

"And in Romania?"

"It's a little harder to be like that here," she said with a laugh.

She took out a tin box with a map of Palestine on it and showed me a slot on top that was for coins. When the box was full, she said, it would be sent to Palestine to buy land.

"How come it's empty?"

She gave it a shake and a few coins rattled inside. "I guess I forget about it," she said.

"Let's hang it in the kitchen and put our spare change in it," I suggested. She agreed to that. She found a good place for it on the wall and went to get a hammer and a nail from my father's tool chest.

"Shouldn't we wait for Papa?" I asked.

"You think I can't drive a nail into the wall? Just watch."

My mother hit the nail on the head and drove it straight into the wall. I was very proud of her. She hung the box. It was too high for me to reach. She said, "If you stand on a chair, you can manage."

Sometimes I would just look at the box and sometimes

I would stand on a chair and drop in the change that had been given to me when I was sent to the grocery store.

One day I asked my mother, "Do the Jews in Palestine have a capital?"

"Of course. It's Jerusalem."

I had heard of Jerusalem from the priest who lived next door.

"Is there a palace there?"

"I suppose so."

"And a king?"

In case you didn't know, before the war Romania was ruled by King Carol, who lived in a palace with his wife, the Princess of Greece, and their son, Michael. Although my mother wasn't aware of it, I was in love with Prince Michael.

"No. Once the Jews had kings too, but they don't anymore."

I thought that was just as well. It was then that I decided Prince Michael and I would go to Palestine after we were married. He would be the king there and I would be his queen.

Whenever I wanted something that I couldn't have right away, I played at it with my dolls. I had lots of them. Most had belonged to my mother, who had gotten them from my grandmother. Although they all looked like little girls, I made one of them my father and one of them Prince Michael. Before I decided to be Queen of Palestine, I always played house with them. I played it with lots of aunts and uncles, some real and some make-believe, who came for visits and had fights and weddings and funerals.

Now that I was going to marry Prince Michael, however, I had a new game. It began with his discovering me. I might be walking in the forest when suddenly he rode by on his horse and noticed me. *Good lord,* he would think, *what a beauty! That's the girl I'm going to fall in love with and marry. When I'm king, she'll live in my palace and be my queen.*

Poor Michael didn't know what he was in for!

Sometimes he would dress up like a poor commoner and go for a walk in our neighborhood. Princes like doing things like that — that's what the books said, anyway. All of a sudden he would see me combing my hair in the window and ask, "Who are you, beautiful maiden?"

"I am Lydia. You have found me at last! How long did you think I was going to wait for you?"

"I've been looking for you everywhere. I had no idea that this was where you lived."

"That's all right. Maybe it was for the best. If you had found me sooner, I couldn't have played this game."

Or else he would drive by with his carriage and footmen while I was out walking with my mother, or maybe just playing in front of my house while watching the people go by. I liked to play hopscotch there, although I was the only girl on the block. He would stop his carriage and say, "Why, that must be the most beautiful girl in the whole world! I'm going to marry her."

At once he would take me to the palace. The palace was usually on my mother's makeup table because of all the pretty bottles there. I would put on her lipstick — not on the dolls, but on myself — and later that night, when the ball was over, I would tell Prince Michael my plans.

"My darling prince, we can't have a church marriage because I'm Jewish and my mother won't let me go to church."

At first he didn't get it. "Jewish?"

"Yes, Jewish. Do you know what that is?"

"Not exactly."

"The Jews are a very ancient people."

"And that's you?"

"Not only me. It's all of us. My father and mother, too."

"You're not Romanians?"

Although I didn't understand it very well myself, I explained that we were Romanian citizens, but that we were also Jews.

"You mean like the Gypsies?"

"What an idea! We're nothing like them."

"Oh. You must be like those Jews in Dudeşti."

"We're not the same at all. Do you get it?"

He did not.

"Some day you will."

"Where are all you Jews?"

"We're scattered all over."

"Then you *are* like the Gypsies!"

"No, we're not, because we have our own country."

And I would climb on a chair, take down the tin box, rattle the coins, and say, "Do you hear that? That's the money we're saving to buy our country back with."

"Where is it?"

"In Palestine."

"Oh. Is that why we shout, 'Kikes, go to Palestine'?"

"Yes. But I still haven't told you that the capital of Palestine is Jerusalem, and there's a palace there but no king."

"I thought — "

"Don't think so much. You'll be the king!"

Naturally, he agreed. If there was still playtime left, I would take all my dolls on a long train trip. I didn't know then that one day I really would travel to Palestine by train. The dolls always fought for the right to sit next to the queen. I made them take turns. In the summer Palestine was out on the terrace, and in the winter it was on the kitchen floor, underneath the collection box, which was filling up. I was sure land in Palestine must be awfully cheap if you could buy it without having to use paper money. I never said that to my mother, though. It would have spoiled the game.

CHAPTER TWO

❧

Kindergarten and "That Woman"

ONE DAY MY MOTHER told me that I would be starting kindergarten the next morning.

"Why?"

"Because I'm too busy to stay home with you all day. You'll spend the morning in kindergarten and we'll be home together in the afternoon."

"Who else goes to kindergarten?"

"Other girls your own age."

"Aren't there any boys?"

"There are boys, too. And there's a teacher and a teacher's helper and lots of toys. The teacher will teach you games and tell you stories. You'll draw pictures, too. It will be a lot more fun than staying home."

"I'd rather stay home and be bored," I said.

"But I'm telling you that I can't stay home with you all the time. You'd have to be here all alone."

"Why can't you?"

"Because I have things to do downtown."

"Like what? Going shopping? Getting your hair done?"

"Lydia, there are things you don't have to know and things you can't understand. Tomorrow you're going to kindergarten. You won't be sorry."

My mother showed me a little straw basket with a lid and two handles and said it was for my snack. All the children brought snacks to kindergarten and ate them at ten o'clock.

"Suppose someone wants to eat my snack?" I asked worriedly.

"No one will," she reassured me. "Everyone eats his own. Isn't this a pretty basket? A real lady's!"

"What will you give me for a snack?"

"Whatever you like best."

Exactly what didn't I have to know, and what besides shopping and hairdos did my mother have to go downtown for? I didn't like the idea, and I went to bed without mentioning it again.

Usually, being bought something by my mother in order to make me do something was enough to make me *not* do it. But the next morning when she packed my new basket with a snack of my favorite salami on a roll, I didn't protest.

Kindergarten started with a prayer, and the teacher was surprised to see that I could make the sign of the cross. I didn't see what was so surprising about it; I had learned it from the priest's children. Then we sat around a long table and were taught how to fold paper into shapes. I wouldn't have minded if we had done it quickly, but there were children who couldn't make the simplest fold and we kept having to wait for them.

After that the teacher told us the story of Hansel and Gretel, which I already knew by heart. I thought my mother told it better, because the teacher said that the wicked stepmother didn't give the children enough food to eat, while my mother said that she didn't give them anything at all and made them look for berries in the woods. The only time she fed them was when their father came home, and then she gave them tiny portions and said as sweet as pie, "The children have just eaten, my dear . . ."

Or take the witch's house. The teacher said it was made out of cake and candy, but I knew from my mother that that was only one wall. A second wall was made out of sausage, a third out of cheese, and a fourth out of bread and rolls, while the roof was made out of ice cream, the windowpanes were made out of Jell-O, and the trees around it were full of fruit and marzipan. Even the flowers were made out of good things to eat, like different flavors of cotton candy.

My mother knew the story a lot better, and the teacher even left out the whole part about Gretel pushing the witch into the oven. All she said was that Gretel gave the witch a shove and ran away with her brother. What she should have said was that Gretel asked the witch as prettily as you please, "Tell me, Mrs. Witch, how do I climb into the oven?"

"You just do, you little dope!"

"But I don't know how to, Mrs. Witch," said Gretel, as sweet as pie.

"Stop calling me Mrs. Witch and get in there!"

"I'd be glad to if only I knew how."

"Bend over. More. More!"

"I'm bending as far as I can. It's just that I can't get my back in . . ."

"Then put your legs in first."

"I'll fall."

"Not both of them at once, you little fool! First one, then the other. One leg at a time!"

The witch showed her how to do it. She put a leg in the oven and said, "Here, look sharp. You do it like this, do you understand? Hey, what are you doing?"

This was where you had to tell how Gretel pushed her into the oven as hard as she could and slammed the door. And how they could hear the witch shouting, and what she said. First there were curses. Then there were promises. Then she begged. Then she screamed so loud that the children ran off to the forest to keep kind little Gretel from feeling so sorry that she would let the witch out. Because witches never felt sorry for anyone, and do you know what would happen if Gretel did that? I'll tell you what: she would never be able to fool the witch again, and the witch would cook them and eat them just as she had planned.

Finally, it was ten o'clock. The story had given me an appetite. The teacher told us to sit down, open our baskets and lunch boxes, spread our napkins, and take out our snacks. When I was finished eating, I said to her,

"Now phone my mother and tell her I want to go home."

"Lydia, what are you talking about? We're having lots of fun and there are still plenty of games to play. And then we'll have arts and crafts."

"No, we won't," I said. "I'm bored. I know all your stories better than you do. I want to go home."

"But your mother told me that the painters were there."

"Then she must be there too."

"You'll go home with the other children at noon."

I began to scream and stamp my feet. I was a good screamer, because I got plenty of practice each time I told the story of Hansel and Gretel to the priest's children and to my dolls. At first the teacher tried calming me. When that didn't work, she and her helper tried stopping my mouth. But if the wicked witch had been as strong as I was, Gretel could never have pushed her into the oven. The other children were frightened and began to cry, and the teacher phoned my mother and told her to come for me.

My mother looked very angry when she arrived. She tried to talk me into staying. "Papa isn't home," she said. "The painters are there and I have a whole lot to do. Be a good girl."

But I didn't want to be a good girl and when my mother saw that I couldn't be coaxed, she dragged me outside and spanked me. I remember even then having the odd feeling that it wasn't just because of the kindergarten. She was having a hard time with my father and needed to get it out of her system. And as if she didn't have enough to put up with from him, here she was getting more guff from me! This wasn't the first time she had lost her temper and hit me, but she had never done it so hard.

I wouldn't give in, though, and in the end my mother had to take me home. All the way there she kept shouting at me, and now and then she hit me again. That was my last day in kindergarten.

"What kind of child are you?" she yelled. "You're uncontrollable."

No one could ever make me do what I didn't want to.

My father was at home less and less. He never came for lunch anymore and often skipped supper too. And after supper he went out and I never knew if he came back that same night. My mother cried a lot, even when there was no special reason. She told me that the fault wasn't my father's but "That Woman's." And once I heard her scream at him, "You're a doormat, a nothing! You do whatever that woman tells you to! If your daughter stays home all day and won't go to kindergarten, you might at least take care of her yourself. She's yours, too!"

One day I heard the neighbors whispering on the stairs. They were talking about my parents. One of them said, "Didn't you know?"

"I can't believe it. He did?"

"Just imagine!"

They exchanged a few more whispers and burst out laughing.

I also heard my mother talking to my grandmother. She said, "He didn't even care for her. She cast a spell over him, that trash from Dudeşti! She couldn't even type. The paper was going to fire her. She phoned everyone

20

she knew — us too. And fool that I was, I said, 'Why don't you help the poor girl? There must be something you can do for her . . .' "

I've already told you that Dudeşti was a poor Jewish neighborhood in Bucharest. My parents and their relatives looked down on the Jews who lived there. They couldn't even speak proper Romanian. I was happy to hear that That Woman came from there. That meant my mother was a lot classier than she was.

The part about her casting a spell worried me, though. Because if she was a witch and could cast spells, my father would think she was beautiful no matter how ugly she really was. She could even make him think she was young when she was old, or convince him that she was one of King Carol's daughters. And then what would happen?

I was beginning to see what my mother meant about there being things I didn't have to know or understand.

CHAPTER THREE

❧⟨✦⟩❧

Nannies 1, 2, and 3, and I Guess Wrong

Although she fought with him about it, my mother couldn't get my father to babysit for me, and since she really did need some free time, the result was Nanny #1. Her name was Fraulein Gertrud and she spoke German and some Romanian. She told me that she came from Germany, which was a country she had loved so much that she would have laid down her life for it. But the Germans had kicked out her father for being Jewish and had begun to pick on her, too. They had even wanted to send her to some bad place, and she had gotten away just in the nick of time.

Fraulein Gertrud decided to teach me manners. She said that a pretty girl like me shouldn't behave like a caveman. "A well-bred young lady washes her hands before meals and doesn't run around the house like a savage. What will happen when you grow up, *liebe* Lydia? No decent man will want to marry you."

"Fraulein Gertrud, I'm not getting married yet. Who

says I'll even want to? If it's so wonderful, why aren't you married yourself?"

"I may not be married yet, but — "

"Just look at my mother. She married and all she does is fight with my father. He doesn't even live at home anymore."

"We're eating our breakfast now, Lydia, not discussing your parents."

"All right, Fraulein Gertrud."

"Fork in your left hand, knife in your right, please."

"How come you never got married?"

Usually she was so happy to tell me her problems that she forgot which of my hands was which. All of her stories began with the same sighs.

"You see, *liebchen,* I fell in love, but when my boyfriend's father found out that I was Jewish he made him stop seeing me. And that was a long time before Hitler . . . Will you please *eat!"*

"You don't have to tell me to eat. I like eating more than you do. I was just listening."

"For that you have ears, not a mouth. It's not my fault that I have to watch my weight. And so I wasn't allowed to see my darling anymore. Do you understand, *liebchen?"*

"Yes, I do, Fraulein Gertrud. And you love Germany and the Germans so much that you were ready to die for them."

"That's so. I was the best pupil in my class. I knew Schiller, Goethe, Heine, by heart. To think of all the poems I knew!"

Here she always stopped her story to recite a poem in

23

German, which I interrupted because I didn't understand a word. I would ask her to sing instead, and she would sing me all kinds of German songs. According to her, they were songs that she had sung when she was my age, but it was hard to think of Fraulein Gertrud being my age, or ever being a small girl at all.

"Ach, yes, I would have died for my country, and just look what they did to me! You should have seen those hoodlums marching in the streets with their swastikas and shouting, 'Down with the Jews!' Ach, yes, *liebchen*, it's open season on the Jews there."

"What did they do to you?"

"They wanted to send me to a very bad place . . . a very, very bad one in Poland. And so I ran away and came here."

"But what did they actually do to you? Did they hit you or pull your hair or something?"

"No, thank God. I got away just in time."

"Then how do you know that that bad place in Poland is so bad?"

"Everyone knows. It's a place no one comes back from, if you know what I mean. Lydia, how can you sit like that? Put your two feet on the floor! Pick up your napkin! Fraulein Lydia, why aren't you drinking your milk?"

"Tell me how you got away."

"How did I get away? Well, you see . . . but just look at how you're drinking! Who taught you to slurp like that? And don't chew with your mouth open like some peasant boy!"

"I wish I was a peasant boy!"

"Lydia, you don't know what you're saying. Would you like to raise pigs and go around in mud up to your knees all your life?"

"I wish I did raise pigs!"

It went on like that every day for three whole months. Lydia, put your feet on the floor! Lydia, stop smacking your lips! Sit up straight, Lydia, do you want to raise pigs?! Keep your mouth shut when you eat, Lydia! The only thing I was allowed to do my own way was swallow.

Whenever we went out, Fraulein Gertrud tried to teach me how to walk. She scolded me if I made faces at anyone. She made me step aside for old people, behave politely in shops, and never, never touch anything in them. She taught me how to curtsy, the way you do to a king or queen. Once we had a visit from some shriveled, old aunt of mine who could barely make it up the stairs. When she stepped into the apartment, Fraulein Gertrud whispered, "Lydia, *now!*"

She taught me to pick up what grownups dropped and hand it back to them politely. Never to throw things. Always to say thank you and please. And of course, to speak German. After three months of this I felt ready to explode. I didn't know what to do. It was worse than kindergarten.

One day I asked my mother to get me another nanny, but all she said was, "Lydia, you already have one and you'll have to get used to her."

Another month went by. I tried talking to my mother again, but she wouldn't listen. My only choice was to declare Fraulein Gertrud an official enemy. I wasn't sure how Ion and Mihai did it, so I gathered all my dolls, sat them on my bed, showed them a drawing I had made with my crayons of Fraulein Gertrud as a witch, and said to them in my deepest voice, "You are my witnesses that I, Lydia Hoffmann, declare this woman to be my enemy!"

And when I had answered "We are your witnesses" for them, I announced, "From now on it's open season on her!"

I wasn't sure just what that meant, but Fraulein Gertrud had told me it was something they did to the Jews in Germany.

"Down with Fraulein Gertrud!" the dolls and I shouted together.

I was extra nice to her when she came the next day, like the witch when she first saw Hansel and Gretel nibbling the walls of her house. "Fraulein Gertrud," I said to her in a syrupy voice, "could you please take me to the amusement park today?"

"Since you asked me so nicely, *liebchen*, of course I will."

I had a plan. At first I behaved perfectly, and Fraulein Gertrud paid for two rides on the merry-go-round and for a stick of cotton candy. Then I climbed onto a high swing that I had spotted earlier and fell off of it on purpose. The idea was to make believe that I had hurt my head, but in the end I hit the ground so hard that I really saw stars. Fraulein Gertrud was terribly frightened and asked a man to help carry me home. I had a big black-and-blue bump on my head. They tried putting cold compresses on it and pressing it with the flat side of a knife, and when it didn't go away they called my mother at the

26

hairdresser and my father at the paper. They both came home and my father shut the door to my room and asked me what had happened.

I said, "She sits in a café with her friends and doesn't even look at me. Some big boy came and knocked me off the swing."

My father left the room and I heard shouts. He yelled at my mother, and my mother said that if he was so smart he should find me another nanny himself. So they fired Fraulein Gertrud and hired Nanny #2. While they were looking for her my mother asked me what had happened on the swing. I told her the truth. When I'm asked, I generally do.

"But why didn't you tell me, Lydia? We could have had a talk with Fraulein Gertrud and worked it all out."

"Mama, I did tell you. I asked you to find me another nanny who wouldn't nag me all the time, don't you remember? And all you said was, 'Lydia, you have a nanny and you'll have to get used to her.' "

"I don't remember."

"Well, you would have if she had been *your* nanny."

Nanny #2 was a Russian aristocrat, a countess or something like that, although she was pretty young. My mother told me that she was a "white Russian" who had escaped from the Communist Revolution. That made me think that all nannies must be escaping from one thing or another. She wasn't so white either, but my mother explained that the Russian aristocrats were called that because they had a white flag and the Communists had a red one. Her name was Mademoiselle Natasha and she knew French, as a Russian countess should. She also played the piano. In exchange for her room and board she was supposed to look after me, take me out for walks, and teach me French, as well as help with the cleaning and the cooking.

The problem was that she was scared to death that something would happen to me. Perhaps my mother had told her about Fraulein Gertrud. She made me hold her hand in the street, and she never took me anywhere interesting. The amusement park, needless to say, was out of the question. We never even went to the zoo. Things were pretty bad. I wasn't allowed to do anything. It was always, "*Non, non, non, ma petite chérie*, you musn't! You're not allowed to cross the street by yourself, absolutely not!"

Or else, "Oh, no, you don't! You musn't turn on the hot water by yourself. You'll burn yourself, *ma poupule*."

Or, "No, no, no! Hold my hand on the stairs and don't run. Never run! Suppose you fell, *ma poussin?*"

"I wish I had!"

"You're lucky you didn't, *ma petite chérie*. Do you know what can happen when you fall?"

One day I began to scream, "Of course I know! I can break my leg! I can break my arm! I can break my head!"

"Lydia, *mon coeur*, please don't shout, you might tear a vocal chord."

"I hope I tear them all!"

You probably think she was a real sweetheart, calling me all those pet names in French. Would you like to know what they meant? They were yucky, my little hen . . . my cricket . . . my baby mouse . . . my tiny bird. And as if it wasn't bad enough that I had to learn to cook and sew, I had to read books and talk French and play the piano, too. "They're all musts," my mother said to me.

A must was a must.

If only she would take me to the zoo, I thought, *a lion or an elephant might eat her for breakfast.* How I would have loved to see a lion gobble down Mademoiselle Natasha!

I tried talking to my mother this time, too. I explained to her how annoying it was to have Mademoiselle Natasha watch me all the time and not let me do anything. But my mother only said, "Lydia, how can you say such things about such a gentle soul? You couldn't ask for anyone more devoted or responsible."

"But Mama — "

"Lydia, I'm telling you to do what she says. Where will I ever find such a cultured nanny who can teach you French and piano and help with the housework?"

"But Mama — "

"Lydia, I don't want to hear another word. She's your nanny, and thank God that I found her."

What else could I do? I declared *her* an official enemy too.

One chilly autumn day we went for a walk. It started to rain and Mademoiselle Natasha wanted to go home, because I easily came down with colds and sore throats. But I didn't feel like going home, and when she tried to make me I slipped and fell into a puddle of water. Of course it was an accident, but once it happened I decided that I might as well get sick for real, so I dug in my heels and refused to budge. The harder she tried pulling me out of the puddle, the harder I clung to trees, lampposts, railings — whatever I could. One man even thought that I was being molested and came over to rescue me. Mademoiselle Natasha began explaining that she was my nanny and that she couldn't understand what had gotten into me, because I had never behaved this way before. But the man wouldn't believe her. In the end she began to cry and he agreed to help her bring me home in order to see if she was telling the truth. My mother wasn't there, but the priest's wife confirmed Mademoiselle Natasha's story.

The next day I had a temperature. It wasn't very high, though, so I stuck the thermometer into a cup of hot tea and showed it to my mother, who was so alarmed that she phoned my father to come home. The two of them sat in the kitchen while I pretended to be delirious and babbled through the open door of my bedroom, "She wouldn't stop . . . she kept talking and talking to that man . . . and all the time I was lying in that puddle . . . ooh, it was so wet . . . I feel so sick . . . oh, I feel awful . . ."

The next day the doctor came, and my mother sat by my bed all day long and read me stories. When I asked what had happened to Mademoiselle Natasha, I was told that she had been dismissed.

Mademoiselle Natasha was followed by a Romanian teenager named Marioara. She was escaping too, although only from her own father, who took all the money she earned. He was out of work and got drunk all the time and yelled at her for dressing like a floozy. Although Marioara didn't live with us, she did housework too when she wasn't taking me out. At least she took me to interesting places. Mostly these were in the red light district, which was called Cruce de Piatra. She gave me language lessons too, and taught me all the Romanian swear words that I didn't know yet. Marioara didn't laugh when I told her of my plans to be Queen of Palestine. She knew that we were Jews and even that Palestine was the Jewish homeland.

"You'll marry a prince there?"

She was a mind reader!

"You bet."

"Do you know what he looks like?"

"How could I?"

"It's simple. Anyone can see what the man she'll marry looks like. Do you want me to show you?"

Of course I did.

She explained what I had to do. "One night when you're alone in the house, turn out all the lights, light two candles, and put them in front of a big mirror like the one in your parents' bedroom."

"Okay."

"After a while," she whispered, as if letting me in on a dark secret, "you'll see a procession of people in the mirror. You musn't talk or even move. They'll go by without seeing you until one of them stops, turns around to look, and comes over. That's the one who'll be your husband."

"You mean he'll step out of the mirror?" I was really scared.

"No." She laughed. "But when you grow up and meet him, you'll recognize him right away."

When my mother went out that evening, I searched all the drawers in the kitchen until I found some candles. Then I took them to her bedroom, opened the big closet, lit them, and stood where Marioara had told me to. At first all I saw in the mirror was myself and the furniture behind me. I thought that maybe I wasn't concentrating enough, so I tried harder and suddenly I saw a man. I was so frightened that I screamed, but it was only my father.

"Lydia, what's the matter? Are you all right? What are you holding those candles for?"

I was too petrified to talk. He blew out the candles.

"Papa, I didn't hear you come in."

"I tried to be quiet because I thought you might be sleeping. I came to get a book of mine."

He took me to my room and put me to bed. I made him stay with me until I fell asleep.

Although there were plenty of other times when I was alone at night, I didn't dare try again. In fact, mirrors in the dark began to frighten me. And not just mirrors either, but anything bright that gave off a reflection — even the window panes.

Marioara had a sweet tooth, and when she had eaten up all the candies and chocolates in the house, she asked me to look for coins in the pockets of my parents' clothes.

If I found any there, we went out to buy ice cream and candy. If I didn't, Marioara told me to look in my mother's pocketbooks. At first I took only coins, but after a while I began to take bills too.

One day my mother counted the money in her purse and was surprised. "Lydia, have you been going through my pocketbooks?"

I told the truth.

"Has Marioara been going through my things too?"

"No," I said, "just me."

She fired Marioara anyway and after that I had no more nannies. Since I still refused to go to kindergarten and my mother wouldn't stay home, I was left by myself for hours on end. I spent part of the time playing with my dolls and part of it looking at old picture books or albums. Sometimes I just sat by the window in the living room and stared at the street, or else went to my father's empty study and made trick telephone calls. The telephone was near the window and from it I could see the windows of all the neighbors who faced the courtyard. One of them was a woman on a lower floor across from us who was always talking on her phone. She always smiled at my father too and stopped to talk to him on the stairs, and one day it occurred to me that she must be That Woman.

I said to my mother, "You're never home. Why don't you write down the phone number of some neighbor I can call if anything happens."

"That's silly. What could possibly happen to you at home?"

"But I'm all alone," I whined.

"If anything happens, you can always call for help from the window, or else knock on a neighbor's door."

"But suppose I can't? Suppose I break both my legs and can't walk?"

My mother laughed. "Whose number would you like?"

"Anyone's," I said. "As long as they're always at home."

In big, clear numbers she wrote down the telephone numbers of two neighbors, one of whom was the woman across from us, and she said, "Lydia, I'm warning you. One complaint that you're bothering anyone on the telephone and I'll lock the door to your father's study."

She went out. I waited to make sure that she wasn't coming back for something she had forgotten then began to carry out my plan. As soon as I saw the woman across from us hang up after a long conversation, I dialed her number. At first I didn't say anything. I could see her shouting, "Hello! *Hello!*"

Just as she was about to hang up, I said in my scariest voice, "You have ten days left to live!"

Then I hung up and watched her say something into the receiver. She stared at it for another minute as if it were alive and put it back in its cradle.

The next day I called again at the same time and said more terribly yet, "You have nine days left to live!"

She slammed the receiver down so hard that the phone would have fallen off the table if she hadn't caught it at the last minute. I couldn't help laughing.

I kept calling every day. When she had only one day left to live I must have gotten careless about disguising my voice, because suddenly she glanced at our window and saw me holding the phone and looking at her. Even then I might have gotten away with it if I hadn't panicked and hung up right away. She heard the click and was knocking on our door a minute later.

"Lydia, open up! I know you're alone and I know that your mother gave you my number. I know it's you. Don't think I'm not wise to you!"

I didn't open the door, but when my mother came home the neighbor returned and told her everything. My mother told her that it wouldn't happen again. As soon as the woman left, she grabbed me and gave me a good licking. It was only when I managed to tell her that the neighbor was the same woman who was making a doormat out of Papa that she stopped hitting me and gave me a hug.

"She isn't that woman," she said, beginning to cry. "I'm sorry I hit you so hard, but sometimes you're really too much for me."

"You don't have to be so sorry," I said. "It sounded worse than it felt."

"Promise me you'll never do it again."

I promised. And whatever I promise, I keep.

CHAPTER FOUR

꒰•❀•꒱

My Dolls and the Queen
of Palestine

I PICKED MY PRETTIEST doll to be me and made her a
crown, because in my games I was now the Queen of
Palestine and Prince Michael was my husband. The doll
who was my father was not a bad man, but he was a
doormat that the doll called That Woman could do what
she wanted with. That Woman was my ugliest doll. I
liked to put her to death. Sometimes I shot her, sometimes
I choked her, sometimes I drowned her, and sometimes
I chopped off her head, just like in *Alice in Wonderland*.

I had one game in which the doll who was my mother
was still a little girl and lived in my bed with her parents
and all her family. My father was a little boy, and he lived
with his family in the double bed in my parents' bedroom.
I made houses and rooms for both families out of pillows
and blankets and all kinds of toys and kitchen things, as
much as I had the time and patience for. If my mother
told me that she wouldn't be back until late, say until the
hour hand on the clock reached eight, I would build

country estates or mansions in wealthy neighborhoods.

I found out soon enough that moving the hands on the clock couldn't make her come home any sooner. All it did was cause her to ask in surprise, "My goodness, what happened to the clock?" Then she realized and had a good laugh.

The two families, in my bed and my parents', were on friendly terms, and I had them visit each other in horse-drawn carriages. I also made them big banquets with servants and lots of courses, at one of which my father and mother met. They didn't get married because they were still children, and by the time they did, the rest of their families had died or left the country. In part this was because I never knew my own grandparents, all of whom, except for one grandmother, had died before I was born, or even my aunts and uncles, who had all gone to live abroad. In part, it was because I needed a lot of the dolls to be servants in the palace I was building on the living-room couch, where my wedding with Prince Michael would take place. Not that I didn't have many dolls, but there weren't enough for both big families and lots of servants.

Whenever anyone in either of the families died, I held a fancy funeral to which everyone came. Afterwards, there was always a banquet. Meanwhile my parents grew up, and when they were old enough I dressed my father in a special suit sewn by my grandmother as a present and my mother in a bra beneath her dress, which I stuffed with absorbent cotton. She had two dresses, a red one with blue polka dots and a white one like a bride's. I married them at a big party, which I managed pretty easily by switching the servants and the family around.

My own birth was a bigger problem. Although I had asked my mother how babies were born, the answer she gave me was so dumb that I knew it couldn't be true. It was the kind of thing that only grownups could think up when they wanted to punish you for asking a good question. She should have been ashamed of herself! I didn't know what to do. Sometimes I had myself delivered by storks, like the ones in stories, and sometimes I had the baby pop out of my mother's mouth after she had overeaten. One way or another, I managed to be born, and then my father went to work at the paper and loved my mother very much until That Woman came along and turned him into a doormat by using black magic.

This was one of my favorite parts. I liked it even better than the funerals. I dressed That Woman in what she thought were nice clothes, although they were really very ugly, and hid my father somewhere in the house — under a bed, or behind the bathtub, or beneath a step in the storage closet. Then I took That Woman and said to her, "Where's Papa? Go look for him, you witch! Do your magic, let's see you!"

The poor witch would look for him all over the house and begin to cry, because she needed to find him. Hadn't I heard my mother say that he couldn't live without her? And don't think that didn't worry me, because it meant I had to keep her alive. Papa mustn't lose her, so even though I wanted to make her go away forever, I had to let her find him. Before she did, though, I made her suffer.

I kept taking her to different places in the apartment and swearing that this time she would find my father for sure. "Here," I'd say, "let me just roll back that rug and you'll see his foot" — but there would be nothing there. I would laugh right in her ugly, pimply, crooked-nosed, thin-lipped face, and she would cry and beg and promise me all kinds of presents if only I would tell her where he was.

"All right," I would say, "I admit that I tricked you, but this time you'll find him, I swear. Let me just move those pillows over there and you'll see him. Why, goodness me! I put him there myself, how can that be? Where has he gone to now?"

To tell the truth, sometimes I felt a little ashamed for not always siding with my mother. After a while, I began to like That Woman a bit — or rather, not exactly to like her, but to take her side too. I don't mean the real woman, just the doll. I would let her say things that sounded as if she meant them, like, "How can you do this to me? Have a heart! Tell me where he is, I beg you . . . pretty please . . . don't you feel the least bit sorry for me?"

If crying didn't help, she would begin to scream and threaten at the top of her lungs until I said, "All right, witch, calm down! Stop screaming. In a minute one of the neighbors is going to want to know what's happening."

In the end I would fling her at my father's hiding place and step on her for good measure.

Sometimes I played that That Woman and my mother met. This always happened in a café that I built underneath the coffee table in the living room. They would start by being on their best behavior. My mother would explain patiently that she loved my father and had a little girl who belonged to him. How could That Woman break up our family? Why didn't she go somewhere else and find herself another man? It was hard to know what That Woman should answer. All I knew about her was what my mother had told me or what I had overheard her telling my grandmother or shouting at my father. I tried to think of what I would say to my mother if I were That Woman, and that was that I loved him, period. What did she care if I went with him to the movies or a restaurant?

But that only made her scream, "My husband spends all his money on you and doesn't give me a penny for the house! He doesn't buy a thing for his wife and poor daughter. We're barefoot, naked, and hungry!"

"*Your* daughter has nothing to wear?" That Woman would answer. "You say she's barefoot? Why don't you tell her to go get the new sandal that she left last summer in the cow shit!"

That was a word I had learned from Marioara.

My mother would be insulted but would try to control herself. She would say hurtful things back, like, "He only makes believe he loves you! He really loves me and Lydia. He's just using you."

Or else, "Just look at yourself in the mirror. Look at how ugly you are! Look at the rags you're wearing!"

"Because that's what your daughter dresses me in," That Woman would reply. "She took the red dress with the blue polka dots that Grandma made me and gave it to you."

40

She was right, but so what? She was only a doll. At this point my mother would accidentally spill coffee on her, and she would be sure that it was on purpose. Or else my mother would say, "You'll go to hell, you witch! And I'll be on hand personally to see you burn."

Sometimes they both grabbed my father and tried pulling him as hard as they could. I would pin all three of them together and let their clothes rip when they pulled. And after that, if I had run out of things to say and my mother still wasn't home, they would begin hitting each other wildly, throwing each other around the room, and screaming so loudly that one of the neighbors would come to see what the matter was.

It's embarrassing to admit it, but sometimes I let my mother die and skipped the funeral and the banquet, because I loved her too much to celebrate. As soon as I was alone, my father came back to live with me. That Woman didn't stand a chance. She would come to cry by my bed, which was where my father and I lived, but it didn't do her any good.

One day I got so mad that I grabbed That Woman and cut off her head with my mother's scissors. My mother was furious when she came home, because she really liked that doll. She didn't know it was That Woman in my games. That was something I had never told her. The doll was an antique, and my mother sewed her head back on even though it was Sunday and Marioara, who was a good Catholic, had said you mustn't sew then. If you did, she had said, God would punish you by making you prick your finger. But I watched my mother sew That Woman's

41

head on, and she didn't prick herself at all. Maybe that was because we were Jewish. I didn't tell her that she should be the first to want That Woman to stay without a head.

Another time my father came by. My real one, I mean. You might have thought it was my birthday from the way he hugged and kissed me.

"Where is your mother?"

"She'll be back soon. What are you doing here?"

"I just thought I'd drop in. Is there anything wrong with that? I missed you. Come, sit next to me. What were you doing?"

"Playing. I'm not allowed out until Mama comes home."

"Playing what?"

"Dolls."

"What were you playing with them?"

"You really want to know?"

He really did. I told him about the two families and their weddings, birthdays, and funerals. The funerals made him laugh. He wanted to know who died. I said, "Everyone, but it's not for real. And sometimes I play you and . . . That Woman."

"What woman?"

"You know. The one whose doormat you are."

That made him angry.

"Lydia, who's been telling you such nonsense?"

"No one," I said, a bit frightened. "I heard Mama telling Grandma."

"What do you play with That Woman?"

"You really want to know?"

42

"Yes, I do."

"But don't be angry."

"I won't."

And so I told him. I said, "I keep telling her that you're over here or over there, but you never are. She always finds you in the end, though, so that you don't have to die."

"Why should I have to die?"

"You mean you don't know?"

He didn't.

"Because you can't live without her."

He laughed. "Who told you that?"

"Mama told Grandma."

Afterwards my mother came home with all kinds of good things to eat and we had a festive dinner. It just wasn't very festive. I couldn't see any special reason for it. I only found out the truth the next day.

"Your father's gone away," my mother told me.

At first I thought it wasn't serious. I guess that's what I wanted to think. "Where to?" I asked.

"Far away. To Palestine. Last night was our farewell dinner."

How could she not have told me? I began to scream, "Why didn't you tell me yesterday? *Why?*"

"Because you have a big mouth and might have blabbed."

"I do not have a big mouth and you should have told me. He's not your father. He's *my* father! Who do you think you are?"

"Don't shout and don't be insolent. All the neighbors

will hear you. If you'll sit quietly for a minute, I'll explain it to you."

I said I'd rather stand.

My mother explained that, besides working for a local paper, my father also worked for a newspaper in London. Now that the Fascists had come to power in Romania, he had to leave before he was arrested. Maybe she was right to have kept it a secret. I really did have a big mouth and gossiped about all kinds of things. For instance, all my friends knew about That Woman and my cutting off her head. Some of them were pretty scared, because they didn't know the head was just a doll's. Let them be scared!

"When is he coming back?"

"He isn't. But if it's safer there than here, he'll send us tickets and we'll join him."

"Can the Fascists come to power in Palestine, too?"

"No. Palestine is ruled by the British. There's a German general named Rommel who is trying to get there, but right now there's no need to worry. He's still far away and the English are strong."

"And Papa will live in Palestine?"

"Yes."

"Good!"

"What's so good, Lydia?" asked my grandmother. "The bad times are just beginning."

She meant for the Jews. She didn't know that I had my own problems, because the Fascists had crowned Prince Michael king of Romania, even though his father was still alive. In case you didn't know, King Carol abdicated in favor of his son and left the country. He didn't do it like

44

my father, who took ~~only~~ one little suitcase. According to my mother, King Carol left in a private train with fifty cars, in which were all his possessions and even his mistress, Magda Lupesco.

That last part interested me most. *Maybe,* I thought, *That Woman is a mistress, too.* Magda Lupesco wasn't Prince Michael's mother. His mother was the Princess of Greece, and Magda Lupesco was just an ordinary Romanian whom King Carol had fallen in love with. And yet it was she he took with him in his train of fifty cars!

"What else did he take?" I asked my mother.

She told me what she had read in the newspaper. In fact, she told me over and over, because I kept wanting to hear it again and again until it turned into a bedtime story. Sometimes my mother fell asleep in the middle, but I always woke her and made her go on, although she knew it so well that she could have told it in her sleep.

". . . And so King Carol ordered a train with fifty cars, and all his servants began to load it with everything in his palace: the royal furniture and the royal horses and the royal wardrobe and the royal towels and the royal guns and the royal swords and the big royal four-poster bed with the royal canopy and the royal paintings with the royal portraits of all his royal ancestors in gold frames and the royal furniture and — "

"You already said the royal furniture."

My mother yawned. "And all his servants . . ."

One thing was for sure. King Carol didn't just up and leave like my father. First he told Prince Michael that he was going.

45

". . . and the servants took their wives and their children and all the suitcases and the Persian rugs and the Chinese rugs and the big chests of silverware and of gold and of pearls and of diamonds and of rings and of towels and of sheets and of curtains and of ties and of suits and of pajamas and of socks and of underwear — "

"Mama, be serious."

"You think kings don't wear socks and underwear?"

She began to joke like that when she grew tired of the story, but she really did like to tell me about Magda Lupesco and what she took in her chests. Besides all her jewelry and fur coats and giant mirrors, there was a whole car with nothing but shoes.

"And that's not counting winter shoes and boots, Lydia. She packed those separately. There were twenty suitcases of her most beautiful shoes, studded with diamonds and rubies and sapphires. And five suitcases just of silk stockings . . ."

When I was a queen, I too would have a car full of diamond-studded shoes and a huge chest for my royal silk stockings.

In any case, the Fascists' coming to power had put an end to my plans for Prince Michael. From now on it was clear that I would have to go to Palestine without him. And yet that didn't mean that I couldn't be a queen there. Of course, only a prince or a princess could become a king or queen, but who said I couldn't become a princess? The first king there ever was didn't come from a royal family.

CHAPTER FIVE

〜⚬❀⚬〜

The War, and Did the Saints Go to the Bathroom?

MY FATHER WROTE to us, but since Palestine belonged to the English, who were now our enemies, he was allowed only twenty-five words on a Red Cross form. There wasn't even a return address. All it said was: "Jerusalem."

"But how can we write him back?" I asked worriedly.

"We're sure to get another letter with his address soon. Meanwhile, why don't you write him and draw him a picture."

"Suppose we don't?"

"Then we'll give your letter to someone who is going there."

I wrote and drew some pictures, but there were no more letters, and no one was going to Palestine because of the war.

What the war did bring were all kinds of cousins I had never seen before. They told us that the Romanian army had taken Bessarabia and Bukovina from the Russians and was expelling and killing Jews there. They had managed to escape to Bucharest, though it cost them a lot of money. My new friend Adriana said they deserved it.

"Why? What did they do?"

"They didn't do anything, but my mother said that the Jews in Bukovina and Bessarabia were helping the Communist Russians."

"How does she know?"

"My uncle is in the Iron Guard."

"That's nothing to brag about. They're a bunch of murderers."

"How do you know?"

I told her.

In January the Iron Guard had staged a pogrom against the Jews in Bucharest and had hung some of those killed on hooks in a butcher shop. An old aunt of my mother's had come to our house and cried and cried because they had killed her son.

"It's a good thing Bernard got away in time," said my grandmother.

Bernard was my father, Bernard Hoffman. I didn't dare ask if the Iron Guard ate the people it hung in the butcher shop, but I was pretty sure no one would eat Jews. And actually there were funerals for all the bodies. I wanted to go, but I wasn't allowed, even though I was already in first grade and had been to lots of funerals with my dolls. I was left home, and after my mother came back from the cemetery with her old aunt and my grandmother, the aunt stayed with us for a week. She sat on the rug in her stockings and cried now and then. My grandmother sat near her in the easy chair.

I asked my mother, "What is she sitting on the floor for?"

My mother explained that this was a Jewish custom when you were in mourning for someone who had died.

"Then why don't you do it too?"

"Everyone does what seems right to him."

Adriana didn't believe the part about the butcher shop. "How do you know?"

"Some people took them down and brought them to the cemetery, and I heard them talking about it. Now do you believe me?"

"But they have such nice uniforms, don't they?"

"Big deal," I said.

"And such a nice name: The Iron Guard." All at once she shouted out loud, "Down with the Jews!"

I yelled at her.

"I wasn't thinking of you, Lydia," she explained. "That's just what they shout. Stop being such a dope. Don't you know you're my best friend? Don't you, Lydia?"

She really was. She knew we were Jews from her mother, and she hadn't meant anything by it. I said to her, "My mother's aunt just cries all day long. Her son who was killed by the Iron Guard was already a grownup, but it doesn't matter if he was big or little. She's still his mother."

"That doesn't mean they don't have nice uniforms."

"I don't care about their uniforms!"

"You do too! Every time they march down the street you run to look. I saw you."

"I do not! I wasn't running. I was walking. And that's just because my mother sent me to the grocery."

"I don't believe my uncle hung anyone in a butcher shop, Lydia. That's a lot of baloney. And anyway, there's a war on and we've got to kill the enemy. That's war."

"I'm not the enemy."

"Maybe you're not, but a lot of Jews are subversives."

She had learned that word from her mother. I used to think that Ion and Mihai were making up the things that could be done to an official enemy, but now I wasn't so sure. As Adriana said: war was war. And none of the grownups seemed to think that anything could be done about it — at any rate, none of the cousins or neighbors I knew. Not even the priest. Not even Prince Michael, whom the war had made king. And certainly not my grandmother, who just sighed all day long and said, "Who knows what's still to come."

Whenever she talked that way, she was thinking of the Jews.

❈❈❈❈❈❈❈

Even before the pogroms in Bucharest I had started first grade. It wasn't like kindergarten. The school was very big, with lots of classrooms, and I was in 1-A. When we went outside for recess I didn't look little at all, though. Lots of children thought I was in third grade and I didn't let on otherwise. My mother bought me a briefcase, a set of pens, and some notebooks, and I had to sit at a black desk with a girl much smaller than I. This was Adriana, who wasn't my friend yet. I was nice to her because she reminded me a little of the daughter of our neighbor the priest. Adriana didn't know anything and couldn't even read or write. Neither could the other children. I had already taught myself to read by looking at the street signs, so reading lessons bored me. The only part I liked was when we were told or read stories, because these were ones I hadn't heard before. Some were about the brave kings of Romania, and others were like the stories that the priest told us in religion class.

At first, writing lessons were fun too, because I couldn't write yet and I liked making the letters. After a while, though, I got the hang of it and lost interest. When you're bored you become a nuisance, and that's what I did. Our teacher wasn't at all strict and never made anyone stand in the corner. She scolded me so gently that it had no effect on me at all. Even when she threw me out of class, she did it quietly. I wouldn't have minded it at all in the hallway if I hadn't sometimes run into the principal, who scared me with his shouts and said he would send for my mother. Yet I wished he would, because the second time that happened, you were suspended for three days, which meant three mornings in bed. I hated getting up in the morning for no good reason, and I kept quarreling with my mother about having to go to school.

The only time I got out of bed without a fight, went willingly, and behaved myself in class was during the first month. And even then it was only because I looked up to the teacher. She was the most beautiful woman I had ever seen, even more beautiful than my mother. She looked like a saint and had the sweetest voice, which I never tired of hearing. She never raised it at anyone either, and she had such clear, blue eyes that I shivered just to look at them. Until one day . . . Well, I happened to be walking down the hallway near the teachers' room when I saw her come out of the bathroom.

She noticed me and asked, "Lydia, why are you staring at me like that? Is anything the matter?"

"Oh, no, ma'am," I said.

But something was. I couldn't believe that she . . . why, she was just an ordinary woman who went to the bathroom like everyone else!

I soon made friends with Adriana and we fooled around together in class, played together during recess, and walked home together after school. We shared all our secrets too and were always in each other's houses. When Adriana told her mother my last name, it turned out that our fathers had worked together for many years on the same newspaper. She lived near me, and at last I had a real friend who could laugh and listen and liked to see me carry on. Even in those days I wanted to be an actress.

Adriana's house had a big cross on one wall and pictures of all the saints. And a Christmas tree, which I went especially to see, because we had never had one in our house. She didn't believe me when I told her that Jesus and Mary were Jews too. She asked her mother about it and informed me, "Jesus was a Jew, but then he was baptized and became a Christian."

"Who baptized you?" I asked her.

"I don't know," she said. "It was right after I was born. I'll have to ask my mother."

She asked her mother about everything. It was one of the most annoying things about her.

"Well, what were you before you were baptized?" I persisted.

She thought about that for a minute. This time she knew the answer by herself. "I was a Jew. Everyone's a Jew until they're baptized, didn't you know that?"

Actually, I didn't.

At the beginning of second grade, I was sick for two or three weeks. Adriana was surprised to see me when I returned to school.

"I'm so glad you're still here!" she called out to me, running to give me a hug.

"Why shouldn't I still be here?" I didn't know what she was talking about. My place beside her had been kept for me and we sat together as we had the year before.

"My feelings were hurt," Adriana said. "I thought you had gone without saying goodbye. I was afraid they'd make someone yucky sit next to me."

"I was sick, that's all," I said. "Where did you think we had gone to?"

"My mother said that your father had sent you a certificate for Palestine and that you had already left."

"Since when?" I asked.

"My father heard it at the paper."

When I came home, I told my mother. She turned pale and ran to the telephone. First she talked to Adriana's mother and then to Adriana's father. I could hear him saying over the phone, "We heard that Bernard sent you a next-of-kin certificate to get an English visa to Palestine."

There was a pause then Adriana's father added, "And since Lydia wasn't in school when the year started, we thought you must have left. It seemed odd to us that you hadn't come to say goodbye . . . but in times like these . . . who knows? To tell you the truth, though, I couldn't understand what made Bernard do it, because the way Rommel is advancing in North Africa he's sure to take Palestine too."

"Well, we're still here," said my mother. I could tell that something was on her mind. When she hung up, she said to me firmly, "Come on, Lydia, we're going to look into this."

We went to an office building that I recognized, because I had been to it on some of my walks with my father, who had lots of business there. I didn't mind going with him because he always bought me a bag of candy and allowed me to eat all of it while I waited for him in a room. When we got there, my mother asked for someone named Lili. The woman at the desk said that Lili had gone to Palestine, and she asked my mother, "You wouldn't happen to be Mrs. Hoffman, would you?"

"No, I would not!" shouted my mother, slamming the door.

I let her calm down, then asked her why she said that she wasn't Mrs. Hoffman. She said to me, "Because that doormat of a father of yours — that nothing — sent the certificate to that woman instead of to us."

"You mean you wanted to go to Palestine?"

"Whatever I wanted was none of her business!"

"But Rommel . . ." I tried reminding her.

My mother wasn't even listening. She was so angry and humiliated that she didn't know what to do. She just kept saying to me, or maybe to herself, "But why should the child have to suffer . . . why the child . . ."

So her name was Lili; now I knew. And Adriana had told me the truth. Back home my mother hugged me and began to cry. She hated That Woman almost as much as I did. I was sure she never would have sewn back the doll's head if she had known who it was.

Suddenly she cheered up and said decisively, "To hell with him! I'll find a way to get us out of here without him."

"Mama," I said, "there's always Rommel!"

"Rommel? What do you mean?"

"Adriana's father said that Rommel will get to Palestine, didn't he, Mama? And if he does, maybe he'll arrest That Woman too."

My mother laughed. She wiped her tears away and said, "Believe me, I'm not crying for myself. I can manage without him. But why couldn't he think of you!"

I felt sorry for her, because I knew that her tears really were for herself. It was like the time Adriana made friends with one of the yuckies and told her all my secrets. I couldn't forgive her, but I kept telling myself, "What do I care? I don't give a darn about her. Just wait until I'm Queen of Palestine!"

Maybe Adriana did it to get back at me for what I did one day in religion class.

We were learning about the saints. I raised my hand, and the priest called on me and said, "Would you like to say something, my daughter?"

"No, Father," I said. "I have a question."

"Ask, my daughter."

"Did the saints go to the bathroom, Father?"

All the children burst out laughing. I really wanted to know, but the priest thought I was a troublemaker and threw me out of class. And a while after that, I was thrown out of school. My mother said it wasn't the priest's fault, because the Fascists had expelled all the Jewish children from public school. To cheer me up, she said, "Don't worry. I'll send you to a Jewish school."

Worry? I was disappointed! Here I had been thinking that I wouldn't have to go to school at all! Wasn't there *anything* good about the war?

CHAPTER SIX

Mister Lupo, and I'm Off to Palestine at Last

WHEN WE RAN OUT of money, we began to sell things. First we sold my father's books. Then we sold his suits and some of the furniture. After that we sold some of the sheets and towels from my mother's trousseau. I felt terrible about them, because they were supposed to be part of my trousseau, too, but my mother promised that she would buy me even nicer ones after the war.

Then we moved to a dingy little apartment at the far end of town. It was next to a movie house, though, and that's how I met my first actors and singers. I don't mean movie stars, either. In those days live entertainers appeared on stage during intermissions. They performed under spotlights in velvet clothes with shiny gold trinkets, and I stared at them in admiration.

I finally got up the courage to visit them backstage, and after that, they let me come to rehearsals. One of them was a fat lady singer with a really pretty face. She wore a red velvet dress with a big spider-shaped brooch on her breast. I couldn't take my eyes off her. The doorman knew me and always let me in, in fact, he even gave me candy. I went to every performance, most of all to see the fat singer. Her best song was "Santa Lucia." I told my mother that she was a famous opera singer. She had such a wonderful voice that I was sure it was true. My mother said, "If she were so famous, she wouldn't be performing during intermissions at the movies."

I was crushed. I couldn't believe that anyone sang better. "Maybe she has to do it because of the war," I said.

"Maybe," said my mother.

"Would you come with me to hear her?"

My mother agreed.

I don't remember what movie was showing, but the entertainers appeared as usual during intermission, and when the fat singer came out on stage in her velvet dress with the spider brooch, everyone broke into applause. I clapped too, as hard as I could, but my mother didn't think very much of her "Santa Lucia." She was more impressed by the pantomimist, who was called "Mister Lupo," because he had been an English teacher before the war. He really did have a nice act. Even though he never spoke and there was nothing on stage, he made you feel that there were people and things all around him.

After the show my mother said, "The pantomimist was excellent."

"And the singer?"

"She wasn't bad. Do you know the pantomimist?"

I told her that I did. I knew them all. "How come you want to know?"

"I'd like to meet him," said my mother. "Can you arrange it?"

"It's no problem bringing you backstage. Do you want me to?"

She did. I wasn't at all suspicious. Between showings of the movie, I took her backstage and introduced her to all my friends — Mister Lupo, too. When he wasn't acting he talked like an ordinary person, but even then he sometimes did funny things that made you laugh.

When I went backstage the next day, Mister Lupo took me aside and asked me about my father. Even then I didn't suspect anything. I told him that my father was in Palestine. Mister Lupo told me that he was Jewish, too. "That's not why my father went to Palestine," I said. "He works for an English paper there."

"You're not Jewish?"

"Yes, we are."

From then on he was especially nice to me and always asked me to say hello to my mother for him. I never did, though, because by now something smelled fishy. Then one day the Fascists broke Mister Lupo's leg in two places, and he couldn't perform anymore. The doorman told me about it at the entrance. I told my mother and added that Mister Lupo had always sent her regards.

"Why didn't you tell me?"

I shrugged.

"Find out what hospital he's in and we'll visit him."

"I don't feel like it."

"All right. I'll find out."

The next day she went to visit him, and after he left the hospital, he began to visit us. He was out of work now, because his leg was in a big cast and he walked on crutches. But the worst part of it was that something inside him seemed to have been broken, too. There was no one between the words anymore, just an ordinary person who talked. All this happened in the autumn, when I was starting third grade. The Jewish school had moved too, and was now located in the central synagogue of Bucharest.

Sometimes my mother called Mister Lupo "Lupo," just like the actors in the troop. I didn't like it one bit. I suppose I was beginning to guess where things were heading. My mother wanted Mister Lupo to give me English lessons. "It wouldn't hurt you to know some English," she said. "It's part of being cultured. That's what they speak in America, too."

"Mama," I asked, crestfallen, "do you mean that after the war we're going to America and not to Palestine?"

"Who knows?" said my mother.

"I'm not going to America," I told her. "In school we're studying Hebrew and learning about the pioneers and the kibbutzim in Palestine. One new language is enough for me. And you yourself said that Palestine is the Jewish homeland and that the Jews there are proud and free. I am not going to America! Even Papa said it isn't true that there's gold in the streets there."

"All right, we won't go to America. But you should still know English, because the British now rule Palestine and that's what the children learn there. Lupo will come here every afternoon to tutor you. I have no money to pay him with, but I'll give him supper in exchange. Did you know that he has no family at all?"

"I did, and I don't care."

"You don't? Your own friend is hurt and can't work, and you don't care?"

"He's not my friend anymore," I said. "He's *your* friend."

"You know, Lydia, sometimes people are in a bad way, and if they can't find someone to help them or encourage them, they give up and die."

"You mean they just stop breathing?"

It was funny to think of it like that, as if people were wind-up toys that suddenly ran down. But my mother was serious.

"Mister Lupo is a nice man. He's a true artist, too. I say that because I know something about these things. People like him break easily, especially when they lose the world of their art. I want to help him, at least until he's better. And he's too proud to accept charity. You know that these are very hard times for us Jews. You may not be so aware of it, because you're only a small girl, but you can certainly see what's happening. I've arranged for him to give English lessons to two of my friends also."

For once I listened, because my mother was talking to me as if to a friend her own age. She didn't do that often, but she could convince me of anything when she did.

Mister Lupo came every afternoon when my mother was out and slowly climbed the front steps on his crutches while I watched through the window. He taught me English reading and writing and some simple conversation, and then, if my mother wasn't home yet, he asked me to bring him the newspaper and left me alone at last. After supper I was told to go to my room while he gave my mother a lesson. This went on for a long time, until one day I saw him grab her in the hall and kiss her as she was walking him to the front door. She laughed and pushed him away, and he wobbled on his crutches and almost fell, so that now she had to grab *him*. When she freed herself this time he didn't fall, because he was leaning against the wall. Suppose he even wanted to marry her?

That was all I needed! I already had one father and didn't want another, and I told my mother that I didn't want Mister Lupo to come anymore or to teach me any more English. I didn't care if he did break. He was broken already.

"You can't always have your own way," my mother answered me. "Instead of hanging out in the street or playing dolls, you're better off learning something useful. And anyway, Mister Lupo gives me lessons too."

"Kissing lessons," I said.

She lost her temper and told me to mind my tongue. I could see that she wouldn't give in, so I decided to take matters into my own hands.

The first thing I did was call a meeting of my dolls and declare Mister Lupo an official enemy. When it came to saving my mother, anything went. I even told Adriana, who agreed with me but was scared. She must have thought that I was going to use poison or something.

I don't know if everyone is like me, but I enjoy saying

scary things. Maybe that's how an actor who plays his part well feels, or someone who tells a funny joke. Telling jokes and scaring people are two of the things I like best.

When Mister Lupo came the next day, I asked him, "Would you like some tea, Mister Lupo?"

He wasn't expecting that, because he had always hobbled to the kitchen and made his own tea while leaning on his crutches. "Do you know how to make it?" he asked.

I'll be you're just as scared as Adriana, because you too think I was going to poison him! Actually, I had a different plan.

"Of course I do," I said.

"Why didn't you ever say so?"

"I didn't want to hurt your feelings."

"Why would that have hurt my feelings?" he wondered.

"Because cripples like to feel that they can do things by themselves."

That made him mad. "I'm not a cripple. You know that my cast is only temporary."

"Sorry," I said.

"As a matter of fact," said Mister Lupo, "I would be delighted if you made me some tea."

I brought him the tea. He took one sip and spat it out, because I had put in two spoons of salt instead of sugar, and he went off in a huff to make his own tea. Then he did something unforgivable: he grabbed me and spanked me on the bottom. When my mother came home I kept waiting for him to tell her about it, but he didn't. Neither did I.

After supper I refused to leave the dining room. At first

63

my mother asked me nicely. Then she tried coaxing me.
Then she threatened to use force.

"But I'm afraid to be left alone in my room," I said. "It's
all the way at the other end of the apartment. I'll go to
your room."

She agreed and even let me leave the door of her bedroom open. I listened to every word they said, and each
time he took her hand and began to whisper, out I came.

The next day I poured glue on Mister Lupo's favorite
chair, but he noticed in time and asked for another chair.
That evening he left after supper without giving my
mother her lesson.

The next time he came, I soaped the kitchen floor.
When he went to make tea, he slipped and fell. It was
pretty awful, especially the thud that he made. I felt so
sorry for him that I ran to help him up. He wouldn't let
go of me even when he was back on his feet.

"Did you put soap on the floor to make me fall?"

I could have said that a bar of soap had fallen by
accident, but I told the truth.

"Why do you do such mean things? I thought we were
friends."

"I do them because I don't want you to come here.
Now let go of me."

But he wouldn't.

"Let go!"

"I'm going to punish you," he said.

"I'll scream for the neighbors."

Just then my mother walked in. "What are you two
doing?" she asked.

"He won't let go of me!" I screamed. "He grabbed me and won't let go! That's what he does when you're not home."

"You little liar," said Mister Lupo.

Although I really didn't like to lie, I had no choice. But my mother didn't believe me, because Mister Lupo told her about the salt and the glue and the soap, which was still on the floor and all over him. Any moron could have seen who was telling the truth, and my mother was no moron. She took me to her room and shut the door.

"Lydia, what's going on?"

"I don't want him to marry you. Don't think I don't know!"

She started to laugh. "Don't be such a dumbbell," she said. "I have no plans to marry him."

"But you let him hold your hand all the time."

"I just want to be nice to him. He's so miserable. If that's too much for you to understand, at least keep your nose out of it."

"If he comes here again, I'll tell all the neighbors what you do."

"You're going to get it! What do we do?"

"Kiss."

"All right. You can stop taking lessons."

"What about you?"

"That's none of your business."

Mister Lupo didn't come anymore. I hadn't expected it to be so easy, and since I thought my mother might have something up her sleeve, I decided to keep an eye on her. At least I had learned some English, although that only came in handy later.

Meanwhile, we moved again. By now we had no money left at all, so we moved in with a rich uncle who let us have a room in his house. Mister Lupo never came to visit, and before long I made friends in the neighborhood. Sometimes we went treasure-hunting in a ruined old building that stood behind my uncle's. You could find all kinds of broken pots, silverware, and rusty cans there, and even whole bottles that could be sold for enough money to buy ice cream. Once we found a bone.

One boy said, "I'll bet it's a dead man's."

"Go on, it's just a chicken's," said a girl.

"Bull," I said. "Chickens don't have such big bones."

"Maybe it's a dog's?"

"I know," said a bigger boy. He spoke very seriously. "It's the man's who lived here. He killed himself."

I never went back there again. Don't think that's because I'm afraid of ghosts. I just don't like stepping on dead bones.

In the Jewish school I wasn't so much of a discipline problem. Maybe that's because classes were more interesting. There were a lot of new things to learn, like all kinds of holidays I knew nothing about and a new language that was spoken by the Jews in Palestine. I wasn't supposed to say "Palestine" anymore either, but "Eretz Yisra'el," which means the Land of Israel. From then on I was no longer Lydia, Queen of Palestine in my games, but Lydia, Queen of the Land of Israel.

On the holiday of Tu B'Shevat, our teacher brought us oranges and raisins from Eretz Yisra'el. She divided the oranges into sections and gave one to each child, on which she put a single raisin. She was one raisin short, because a girl had stolen and eaten it. My friend Sarah and I saw her and told on her. The teacher asked us to come out to the corridor and said, "Please, I don't want anyone knowing about this. That girl comes from a very poor home and probably never ate a raisin in her life."

We promised to keep it a secret, and we did. That is, we told all the other girls in the class, but we made them swear not to breathe a word of it.

The best parts of school were the choir and the plays that were put on by the children on a real stage, with the parents in the audience. I was still new when the choir performed on the birthday of Theodor Herzl, the prophet of a Jewish state. At the last minute one of the soloists got sick and the music teacher frantically looked for a replacement. I volunteered and was asked to sing something. I sang:

"San-ta Lu-cee-ee-yah . . ."

"I'm very sorry," said the music teacher, "but I can't use you as a soloist. What is your name?"

I didn't answer. I wanted to, but I couldn't get the words out. I felt the blood drain from my head and I passed out, although I didn't realize I had until I opened my eyes and found myself lying on the floor, surrounded by anxious teachers and students. They probably thought I was dead. I wished I were. Me, not good enough to be a soloist? What an insult!

That was the first and last time in my life I ever fainted. My friends thought it was just an act. I told them they were right, because I couldn't bring myself to admit that being turned down by the music teacher had had such an effect on me.

To tell the truth, I may not have sung that well, but I didn't sing that badly either. And in the end I swallowed my pride and joined the choir when I was asked to. Maybe that's why the music teacher had wanted to know my name. I also tried out for a play that the drama club was staging about the pioneers in the Land of Israel, and despite my fears of rejection I landed the lead part.

That was when my mother chose to inform me that I was going to Palestine myself.

"But I have the lead part in the play!" I said.

"They'll find someone else."

"When are we leaving?"

"Lydia, I have to tell you something. You're going with a group of other children. I'll come, too, but later."

"How are we going?"

"By train."

"Don't tell me there's no room on the whole train for you, too, Mama."

"You don't understand, Lydia. The Germans won't let me out. I'll have to cross the border illegally. I know a fisherman who smuggles Jews to Turkey. He's ready to sail as soon as the weather is better."

"Then I'll come with you!"

"You can't. It's a difficult trip and he doesn't want any children or old people."

I thought my mother was pretty old herself, but I wasn't going to argue about that. "Where will I live until you get there?" I asked.

"We're a group of five grownups. We're in touch with a secret agent from Palestine and he's arranged for us to go to a kibbutz called Tel Harish. Someone from the kibbutz will come to pick you up when you arrive. You have nothing to worry about. You'll start school right away and I'll join you as soon as I can."

"What's a kibbutz?"

"It's a sort of pioneer village where everyone lives together and shares things. Didn't you learn about kibbutzim in school?"

I remembered that we did. I just hadn't paid much attention to it.

"And the other children?"

"They'll all go to some kibbutz or boarding school."

"How come we're going now?"

"I've been trying to arrange it for the past half a year, but I never told you about it. I wasn't sure that anything would come of it, so why excite you for no good reason?"

"Is that why you wanted me to study English with that man?"

"Please do not call him 'that man.' Yes, that was why. And it's too bad you stopped."

"I'm not going without you!"

My mother wrung her hands, making the cracking sounds with her knuckles that my father and I both hated.

"Lydia, you have to realize that this is a special arrangement for a small group of Jewish children. It took all the connections I have. I don't know what's going to happen in this country. Things are getting worse and worse. There are rumors that . . . that in some places the

Germans have begun murdering all the Jews. We have to get out of here. I could have arranged to be smuggled out long ago, but I had no solution for you. This is our one chance. You'll have to go without me, but it will be an easy trip and I'll come as soon as I can. I promise you."

"Suppose no one from the kibbutz comes for me?"

"Don't worry. You won't be abandoned. You'll be taken care of until I come."

"Suppose Rommel gets me?"

My mother laughed. "Rommel won't get you, Lydia. The English have already driven him back."

"I wish they hadn't," I said.

"How can you say that? Rommel almost conquered Egypt and Palestine. God knows what Hitler would have done to all the Jews there . . ."

The real reason was that in one of my games there was a doll named Rommel who got hold of That Woman and shook the living daylights out of her.

"But I can't go. I have the lead part in the play."

"Believe me, Lydia, this is far more important than any lead part in any play. Lots of mothers would give their right arms to get a place for their children like the one I got you."

"Mama, I don't want to go without you!"

"You have to. It's a matter of life and death. It's not a game this time."

"But what will we do if Papa is still with That Woman?"

My mother stared at me for a moment and said, "Of course he's still with That Woman. But we're not going to Papa. That's not why we're doing this. We're going to a kibbutz, do you understand?"

"Suppose I bump into him in the street?"

"I don't know, Lydia. You'll have to do what seems right to you. I'm not sending you to Papa. He doesn't deserve a wonderful child like you after all he's done. But he is your father. If you want to look for him while you're waiting for me, I can't stop you."

"You mean you won't look for him when you come?"

"I certainly will. And I intend to settle a few scores with him."

"What kind of scores?"

"Sending That Woman our certificate."

"And you'll settle a few scores with her, too?"

"I don't care about her anymore."

"Don't you hate her?"

"I do, but I'm not going to give her the satisfaction of knowing it."

Although I didn't tell my mother, I decided that she could leave that to me. If I managed to find my father, That Woman would feel sorry I did. Once she was out of the way, Papa and Mama could live together again.

My mother must have sensed that I was planning something, because she said, "Lydia, don't say anything about Papa on the kibbutz."

"Why not?"

"I have my reasons. I'll let you know what they are when I get there."

She wanted to say something else, but she didn't. She just hugged me, with tears in her eyes.

71

CHAPTER SEVEN

*Sixty Meatballs, and On Not
Being a Sore Loser*

To TELL YOU THE TRUTH, I was scared. I could see
that my mother's mind was made up, and that she
was going to put me on the train even if I had to be
dragged there. And there wasn't much time to think of
a way out, because in two days I was supposed to be at
the train station with a blanket, warm clothes, and enough
food for three days. My first plan was to run away and
hide until the train pulled out. The more I thought about
it, though, the more it occurred to me that the trip might
be fun. Traveling to a faraway country was like an ad-
venture story. I decided to go.

My mother did all the preparations. We were too poor
by then to afford any special treats. When she asked what
I wanted to take along to eat, I said, "Meatballs."

My mother made wonderful meatballs. This time she
made sixty of them, wrapped them in wax paper, and put
the wax paper in a little, blue pillowcase. She also gave
me some fruit and some cornbread. For the past two years,

all the good things had been gone from the shelves in Romania. I hadn't seen a piece of cake in ages. And yet my mother did give me a bag of dry cookies and some sucking candies and chocolates. Perhaps she had put them away in better times.

The day arrived. I was supposed to be at the station in the early afternoon. The train was leaving at four o'clock sharp. My mother got hold of a knapsack and managed to fit everything into it except for the blanket. She washed my hair and gave me a new dress to wear that was a present from my grandmother, who had sewed it especially for my trip.

"Grandma, how did you know I was going?"

"I've known for half a year."

Everyone knew but me! I gave her a big kiss. Although she had been sick for the last month, she came to our house to see me off. It really was a nice surprise.

The closer it got to leaving for the station, the more nervous my mother became. She kept wandering around the house and doing all kinds of pointless things. I packed my dolls in a separate bag.

"Lydia, it's time to go."

My mother wrapped her bright scarf around my neck and helped me into my coat, even though these were things I had learned to do by myself long ago. She also gave me my documents — that is, my birth certificate and my last report card — and handed me an empty envelope with an address in Turkey on it.

She sat with me on her lap, hugged me tight the way she used to when I was little, and said very seriously, "As

73

soon as you get there, write to me right away. And I mean *right away*, Lydia, do you understand? I want to know that you're okay. Make sure to tell the kibbutz that the letter goes to Turkey. From there it will get to me in Romania, is that clear? Do you promise? I want you to know, Lydia, that your grandmother and I won't have a moment's peace until we hear from you."

After I promised, she hesitated for a second, then gave me a photograph. It was of her and my father on their wedding day. They were dressed like a bride and groom, and they had their arms linked and were smiling. I felt those smiles were for me, even though I knew they were just for the photographer.

I never understood how people could fall in love and get married and then fall out of love. I was sure that when they took that picture, my mother would never have called my father a doormat and my father would never have had another woman. When I fall in love it will be forever, even if it isn't with a prince. No one will take my husband away from me!

Last of all, my mother handed me my father's letter from Palestine. "If you ever want to look for him, this letter may help you."

"Mama, you told me — "

"I know. But you never can tell."

"You mean you may not come?"

"Lydia, I'll do everything humanly possible to get to you as soon as I can. But you know that there's a war on. Anything can happen. Don't worry, though. Nothing bad will, and I'll get there safely."

Over a hundred children were in the train station, all with knapsacks and bundles. I was the only one under thirteen, but you would never have guessed I was only ten from looking at me. Some of the children came with mothers and grandmothers, some with both parents, and a whole lot in groups with counselors. That's when I found out that everyone but me belonged to some organized group.

My mother took me into one of the train's cars and seated me in an empty seat. All the window seats were taken. I didn't cry until the whistle blew and she had to get off. Everyone else who had to say goodbye to someone was crying too. I hugged her hard and barely listened to all the last-minute things she was telling me, like what to eat first, and what to eat last, and not to sit on the meatballs.

Afterwards I saw her with the others, waving from the platform as we pulled out. I waved back as hard as I could. Even when we had left the platform far behind, I still thought I could see her.

I glanced at the boy next to me by the window. He glanced back. I took out my meatballs and ate one.

His nose twitched. "Is that real meat?" he asked.

I could see that the other children were listening. In those days most "meatballs" were made from vegetables. I told him these were real. "Would you like one?" I asked.

He said he would.

"Then change places with me."

He thought it over then said, "Just for today."

"No," I said. "For the whole trip."

"One meatball isn't enough."

"I'll give you one each day."

"No," he said. "Two each day."

I pretended to think it over, then agreed. The other children were jealous, but I wasn't about to give out free meatballs. Who knew what else I would need them for during the trip?

We began to talk. A girl asked me what group I belonged to. All the other children in my car belonged to the Young Pioneers. I said I didn't belong to anything. They knew a lot more about Palestine than I did. All I knew about were Herzl and the blue-and-white collection box.

After a long while it began to get dark out. I wondered what had happened to all the grownups who were supposed to look after us. My mother had said that they were only on the train because of connections or bribes. I asked the other children. The boy I had changed places with laughed and said, "They're all making out in their own car."

"They're busy smooching," said the girl across from me. "They don't even care about us."

Although I wasn't sure exactly what that meant, I got the general idea. And maybe it was just as well that we were left to ourselves. The other children may have known things that I didn't, but they weren't very practical. When everyone began to yawn, one of them suggested taking out our blankets and going to sleep. They all thought they would sleep sitting up. Not me, though.

I paid two of them three meatballs each to sleep on the floor, and I had a whole bench to stretch out on.

The next day we changed trains in a city in Bulgaria. Our counselors appeared to take us by groups for a tour of the city. The problem was that we had to take all our things with us. Some children preferred to stay behind in the waiting room, but I decided to go along.

Bulgaria didn't look any different from Romania. The food wasn't any better either. Suddenly, I passed a store window in which I saw some luscious-looking pastries with whipped cream and custard. I asked the others to wait while I went inside and pointed to the pastries. Then I showed the saleswoman the contents of my knapsack. When she went through it and didn't want anything, I offered her my mother's scarf. I was sure that Palestine would be too hot for scarves anyway. She felt it and asked in sign language, "How many?"

I held up six fingers. She only wanted to give me four pastries. I wouldn't back down. Neither would she. In the end I started to walk out and she agreed to five. She laughed and gave me a slap on the back and said something in Bulgarian. I smiled back. I was very proud of the bargain I had driven.

I decided to share the pastries with the others in my group. There were nine of us — seven children from my train compartment, our counselor, and me — so I gave each half a pastry and kept a whole one for myself. Not that I owed them anything, but five pastries were more than I could have managed to eat. You know what, though? The whipped cream wasn't real whipped cream and the custard wasn't even real custard. It was something I had never tasted before, although later in Palestine I ate lots of it. There, it was called margarine.

After the pastry shop there were the usual things that you saw in a big city, until we came to an ice-cream stand. Wow! It was still early spring and pretty cold (the year, in case you didn't know, was 1943), but I wasn't going to pass up the chance to eat ice cream. It came in scoops and cones just like in Romania, and I offered the woman selling it the woolen socks in my knapsack. At first she thought I wanted to swap them for a single cone, but when I pointed to all of us, she refused.

That's when I remembered the meatballs. I took out the bag and opened it in front of her. First she smelled them. Then she tasted an eentsy bit of one. Then she thought for a minute and agreed: one meatball for one ice-cream cone. But I was getting too low on meatballs to afford that many, so I closed my bag and started to go. If only I had been alone, or with just one other boy or girl — what a feast we could have had! It would have been like the good old days with Marioara. By now everyone wanted ice cream, though. The children shouted and begged and said they would let me have the best window seat and all the food I wanted to eat and benches to sleep on if only I would buy them all ice-cream cones. Even the counselor promised to bring me hard-boiled eggs from the grownups' car, with salt.

I gave in. We all had ice cream, then I went back and bought one more cone for myself with my last meatball.

When we returned to the train station, there were Germans there. We were all scared — the grownups too. These weren't the Iron Guard, who you could try to outtalk in Romanian; they were real Nazi soldiers, with a picture of a skull on their sleeves. They lined us up in groups and asked for our papers. After they checked them all, they took two boys away. The boys cried, but the Germans didn't care. When one of the boys dropped something and wanted to go back for it, a German pushed him so hard that he nearly fell on his face.

We boarded a new train. The grownups saw to it that we stayed in the same groups. I was given a window seat, and our counselor came with enough hard-boiled eggs for everyone. Even though I only got one egg, I didn't say anything. I was thinking of the boy pushed by the German. I wondered if he had a father and a mother, and where they were. I asked the counselor why he was taken away. He said, "The two of them had Polish documents. Only Romanian children were let through."

"What will happen to him?"

"He'll be sent back to Poland."

"All by himself?"

The counselor nodded. He looked very serious. I didn't ask any more questions. I didn't want to know. Everyone said that the Jews in Poland were being killed. I couldn't stand thinking of those two boys with their coats and bundles being killed. This wasn't some game. It was for real. And no one would even be with them.

The train crossed the border into Turkey. We stopped in Istanbul. You could tell right away that there was no war here. The first thing I saw was an old woman selling bananas in a big basket. As soon as we got off the train I headed straight for them. I offered her all kinds of things for them, but she just kept shaking her head. I showed her a little box with some Romanian money in it. She looked at it and laughed. She probably wouldn't even have taken meatballs, but I was all out of them anyway.

All the while a Turkish policeman was looking on with a smile. Suddenly I remembered that I had my father's fountain pen. Since the banana woman only spoke Turkish, I turned to the policeman and tried talking to him in the French I had learned from Mademoiselle Natasha, and when he didn't understand, in the German I had learned from Fraulein Gertrud. That did it! He took the pen and bought me two kilos of bananas. Everyone went wild.

Istanbul was like Bucharest before the war. We were welcomed by the Jewish community and paraded, with our bags, a long way from the train station to a hotel, where we were divided into separate rooms for boys and girls. Suddenly I realized how much I had missed a real bed and real food, served on tables with real silverware and real napkins.

After Turkey came Syria. Although we stopped in a large city there, too, we didn't get off the train. Some British soldiers came to the platform and handed out long, crisp rolls that made a popping sound when you bit into them and were filled with salty white cheese. They also gave us tea with milk in tin army mugs. The rolls were delicious, but I poured out the tea onto the tracks.

We passed through Lebanon until we came to a place called Ras-en-Nakura. That was where Palestine started.

I looked out the window. I wanted to feel excited, but there wasn't even a border that you could see. And it was just an ordinary-looking country with dirt, rocks, and bushes — none of which were made of tin. *What a jerk you are, Lydia*, I thought. It was all because of that tin collection box in our kitchen.

The train kept traveling along a seashore, but I wasn't allowed to sit by the window anymore. My meatballs had been forgotten. The ice-cream cones too. "That's all over with," I was told when I reminded everyone of their promise. Well, maybe for them, but not for me. I knew that boys went to the bathroom more often than girls, so I waited patiently until a boy by a window had to go, and I grabbed his seat right away. I was determined not to budge from it, and when he came back and tried pulling me up, I punched him in the face. He was more startled than hurt. Boys think that if you're wearing a dress, you'll never stand up for your rights.

"I bought ice cream for all of you and you promised," I said. "Now no one is going to make me move."

The other girls took my side. It was four against four. One of the older girls had a window seat herself.

"If you're so smart, give me *your* seat," the boy who went to the bathroom said to her.

She thought a minute and said, "I'll tell you what. Let's take turns."

"Count me out," I said. "When you needed me, you made all kinds of promises. Now keep them. In the Land of Israel, you're not supposed to lie."

I was really mad. The big girl and the boy tried dragging me from my seat. I began to kick and scream and punch whoever came near me. More children came running from other parts of the car. That made me scream even louder. In the end, they let me stay put. Of course, I knew that someone would take my seat as soon as I had to go to the bathroom myself, and that's exactly what happened. I pretended not to care and went to sit somewhere else. No one likes a sore loser. That's what the winners say, anyway.

After a few hours we reached a small station where we were told to get off with all our bags. The train stopped and everyone sang *"Hatikvah,"* the Jewish anthem. I already knew the words by heart from school.

From the station we walked to some long rows of cabins. There were Englishmen in uniform everywhere. Some had rifles, but they didn't wear skulls on their sleeves. And they smiled at us. Of course, the Iron Guard used to smile at us in the street too, but that was only because they didn't know we were Jewish.

The Englishmen brought us to a large dining room. The tables were set, and what most caught my eye were the big pats of butter. I reached for a piece of bread, smeared it with butter, and took a big bite out of it. What a comedown! It tasted like the custard in Bulgaria. I kept on eating, though. As I said, no one likes a sore loser.

CHAPTER EIGHT

∽✦∾

I Arrive in a Strange Place

THE NEXT DAY all the children were assembled in a large room, and different people arrived to take them away in groups. I was beginning to worry that no one had come to take me when I heard my name called.

It was a woman from Kibbutz Tel Harish. Her name was Miriam, and she was big and fat. I happen to like fat people. They're never in a hurry, they enjoy eating, and they're not so quick to lose their tempers.

She introduced herself in Romanian. "I'll look after you on the kibbutz until your mother arrives," she said. "Where is your father?"

"We don't know."

Since she had no more questions, I asked, "What is there to eat on the kibbutz?"

That made her laugh. "You'll see for yourself. Are you hungry now?" Instead of waiting for an answer, she handed me a bar of chocolate.

"Can I eat it all?"

"Yes. I brought it especially for you."

I ate the chocolate on our way out of the room, while the other children stared jealously at me.

I was very polite until Miriam told me, "You don't have to call me 'ma'am.' In Hebrew we call people by their first names, and we workers and kibbutz members add 'Comrade' when we want to be more formal. Do you understand that, Lydia? And of course, we'll have to find a Hebrew name for you."

"A Hebrew name?"

"Yes. Everyone at the kibbutz has one."

She didn't look like a worker to me. She looked more like a badly-dressed clerk. And no one was going to change my name. I didn't tell her that, though. I didn't want to start out on the wrong foot.

"Comrade like in Russia?" I asked about this strange way of saying "Mr." and "Mrs."

"Yes," Miriam said. "We're great admirers of Soviet Russia and Comrade Stalin, and of his brave fight against the Germans."

"He's not the one who's fighting," I said. "The ones getting killed are his soldiers."

"Who told you that?"

"My grandmother."

"Naturally, he's not fighting physically, because he's the commander of the Red Army. But he grieves for every Russian soldier who is killed, I promise you."

"My grandmother says he's just another rotten Christian and no better than Hitler."

Although I could tell by her face that Comrade Miriam was shocked, she didn't say anything.

We took a long ride on a bus that stopped in every town and village. Some of the passengers were Jews and some were Arabs. The Arabs spoke Arabic and I couldn't understand them at all, but I couldn't understand the Jews much better. It was only when they spoke slowly or said just a few words at a time that I caught on. I felt glad then that I had paid some attention in Hebrew class.

After a long while, we came to a large city. Comrade Miriam told me that it was Tel Aviv. She had business in all kinds of offices, after which we went to look at the sea. The beach was very nice, with golden sand and a hot sun. When I said that it had been cold in Romania, she launched into a long explanation of the climate in Palestine. She liked to explain things. She explained that Tel Aviv was the first Jewish city and that it was built entirely on sand. She must have been exaggerating, because I didn't see any sinking houses.

The houses did look different from ours, though, and there were street-corner stands that sold drinks made with syrup and soda water. For lunch Comrade Miriam bought me something called a "falafel."

After leaving the beach, we saw a big crowd. A policeman had arrested someone, who kept shouting at the top of his lungs, "I'm an illegal immigrant! I'm an illegal immigrant!"

Everyone was yelling at the policeman, who couldn't

get a word in. Finally a few young men elbowed him aside and freed the arrested man.

The man had just run off down the street when an older man came up all out of breath and cried, "Stop him! He's a thief! He's a thief!"

"I told you so!" the policeman yelled angrily. "Do you think I'd arrest an illegal immigrant?"

The crowd that had set the thief free slunk away shamefacedly. We walked off too. Miriam explained that the British government hunted down Jewish immigrants who entered Palestine illegally, and that the Jews in Palestine tried to hide them and help them get by. It seemed strange to me that the British wouldn't let Jews into their own homeland, but I didn't ask why that was. I had heard enough long explanations already.

We went back to the bus station and took another bus to the kibbutz.

The kibbutz was very pretty. It didn't look like a Romanian village at all. Everything was very orderly, with white houses and red tile roofs and lawns between the houses. And signs everywhere. I tried reading them but couldn't make them out. Miriam explained that they said, "Keep Off the Grass."

"If you have to keep off it, why do you have so much of it?"

"To make the kibbutz beautiful. And you're allowed to lie on it, although not when it's just been watered, because that isn't good for it."

She brought me to the children's dining room, where I ate supper by myself because everyone else had already eaten. The tables had been cleaned, and some boys and girls were mopping the floor. I sat in a corner while Miriam brought food from the kitchen. There was real butter at last and a fried egg. I asked for seconds and got them. Miriam told the kitchen staff that I was hungry from the trip. Starting tomorrow, she explained, I would live in the children's dorm, but it was too late to make arrangements now so I would spend the night with her.

Miriam had a single small room with lots of books in Hebrew and Romanian. Under her bed was another bed on wheels. She pulled it out and made it for me. Before I knew it, I was awake again and it was morning.

It might have been the creaking of the door that woke me, because Miriam had just come in. She was holding a bundle in her hands. "I brought you some clothes from the children's storeroom," she said. "I hope they fit. If you wear that dress of yours, the children will laugh at you. We dress differently here."

She handed me a pair of shorts with elastic at the bottom, a sweater, and a shirt. The sweater was light blue and the shorts and shirt were a faded khaki. She also gave me socks and sandals.

"I took your shoes with me to the storeroom to make sure I had the correct size. Is everything all right?"

Everything was all right. She brought me a tray with my breakfast and I sat down to eat.

"We usually don't eat in our rooms," she explained. "Only in special cases, or if someone's not feeling well. But you were sleeping so soundly that I didn't want to wake you. The children have already eaten; they have breakfast after their first lesson. It's ten o'clock. You must be exhausted from your trip."

I didn't tell her that I always liked to sleep late.

Miriam took me to the school and brought me to the teachers' room, in which a man and a woman were waiting for me. One was Comrade Dina, who was going to be my teacher. The other was the headmaster, Comrade David. Miriam hurried off to work. "I'll see you at four," she said. "Come to my room. If you can't find it, the children will show you the way."

She left me with Dina and David, who told me to sit down and asked, "What's your name?"

I told them. Dina said, "There's no such name in Hebrew."

"Well, it's my name," I said indignantly. What kind of welcome was that?

"Let's think of a Hebrew name beginning with 'L,' " Dina said.

"My name is Lydia," I said. "The only person who can change it if she wants to is my mother."

David whispered something to Dina and they decided to let it drop.

"How old are you?"

"Ten and a half."

"And what grade were you in?"

"Third."

"*Third* grade?"

They couldn't believe it. My Hebrew was pretty bad and they thought I hadn't understood the question. I did my best to explain that in Romania you didn't start first grade till the age of seven. Even then they were doubtful, so I said I would bring them my birth certificate and report card.

I went back to Miriam's room. Although I lost my way a little, I found it in the end. When I got there I realized that I didn't have a key, but the door was open.

I returned to the school. Dina and David were waiting for me. They looked at my documents. David said, "You're too big for third grade. And we don't have a fourth grade; we're a small school. How about starting you in fifth grade?"

"Fine," I said. "Miriam forgot to lock her door. Maybe you should tell her."

"We don't lock doors on the kibbutz," said Dina. "We don't have any thieves."

"And no policemen either?"

They laughed. "If there are no theives, there's no need for policemen."

I felt sorry for the children. I'll bet they don't even play cops-and-robbers, I thought. But I was wrong, because they did. It turned out that they played the same games I did.

"We'd like to ask you a few questions," said David.

"Fine."

They tested me in arithmetic and I knew all the answers. I knew most of the answers in English, too. They couldn't test me in French or German, because they didn't know any. Or in Romanian. Then they asked me about the history of Greece and Rome and ancient Egypt, about which I didn't know very much. And although I knew the stories of the Brothers Grimm and Hans Christian Andersen, they weren't interested in them. Fairy tales never count in school. They did ask if I had studied Bible stories, and I told them that I had just a little.

In the end it was decided that Dina would give me Hebrew lessons every afternoon and that I would make up the rest by myself. I told them I could do it. "If we but will it, it can be," I said in my best Hebrew, quoting Herzl. They thought that was very funny.

Dina was the fifth-grade teacher and she took me back with her to her classroom. There was a racket going on as we approached, but it didn't scare me. I was sure that the children would be the same as in Romania. A boy looked out the window and shouted, "Here comes Dina! Here comes Dina!"

Everyone quieted down. We entered the room. The children sat in pairs at school desks, the boys with boys and the girls with girls. There were a few whispers and snickers when Dina introduced me, but she called for silence and sat me next to a single girl. Her name was Ruti. There had been eight boys and seven girls in the class, and I made it eight and eight.

Although I couldn't follow the lesson, I understood enough of it to know I needn't worry. I had always been a good student, and Ruti tried to help me and make me feel we could be friends. And even if Dina didn't seem very nice — she was thin and hard-faced, and the children were afraid of her — I saw after a while that she tried to be fair and wasn't easily fooled. She taught us everything but English and arithmetic. Arithmetic was taught by David and English by a woman who came to the kibbutz twice a week and wouldn't talk anything else to us.

I liked the boys. I think they liked me right away, too. During recess we all went out and sat on the front steps. The little lawn in front of the classroom was too wet to lie on, but the steps were warm from the spring sun. The sun warmed my sweater, too, and it felt good to be sitting there with everyone. One of the boys brought some oranges and Ruti showed me how to eat the white fuzz on the inside of the peels. She also made scary teeth with the peels and made me laugh.

The day in school passed quickly. Everything was new and I had no time to be bored, because I had to concentrate as hard as I could.

After lunch I met the person who was to become my first kibbutz enemy: our housemother, Leah. Although she had already introduced herself in the dining hall, I hadn't paid any attention to her. Now she told me to bring my knapsack of clothes to the storeroom. She explained to me where it was and said she would be waiting for me there.

"Is that where all the clothes are kept?" I asked.

"Yes," she said.

I brought everything I had. She went through it all, looked for a minute at my good dress, and said, "This is a city dress. We don't wear such things. And anyway, we share all our clothing. I'll take all your clothes and add them to the pool."

"Oh, no, you won't!" I said. "I want to have my own clothes and wear what I want to."

"And what will you do when they get dirty?"

"What does everyone else do?"

"Everyone else brings them to the laundry."

"Then so will I."

"But our clothes don't have anyone's name on them. The housemother gives them out according to size."

"That's no problem," I said, "because my clothes are my size."

Leah took my clothes without further comment. I decided to wait and see. I felt bad about the dress, though.

She handed me some underwear and a towel and asked if I had a comb and toothbrush. I did. She also gave me a bar of soap, a soap case, and some toothpaste, and she said, "Spread the toothpaste lightly over half of the brush, once in the morning and once at night. This tube has to last you for two weeks. If it doesn't, you'll have to use soap. We're not millionaires. Now come and I'll show you your room."

I didn't hate her yet. I knew she had to tell me what the rules were. I took my things and followed her to the dorm.

Every class in school had its own dormitory. Mine had five rooms: two for the boys, two for the girls, and a sickroom. A long, hallway-like porch ran along one side of them. There was a shower and toilets, but no signs that said "Boys" and "Girls."

My classmates were in their rooms. One room had three girls in it: Leah's daughter, Ofra, and Ada and

Penina, who were friends. (I had already noticed in class that they giggled and told each other secrets all the time.) There was a fourth bed in the room, but the three of them didn't want a new girl and started to argue with Leah.

"Either Lydia gets the fourth bed," said Leah firmly, "or one of the girls from the other room does, and Lydia moves in there."

"Which girl?" they asked.

Leah went to get the other girls. The only one ready to switch rooms was Ruti.

"It's either Lydia or Ruti," said Leah. "Take your pick."

To my surprise, they chose me. Maybe they thought Ruti was yucky, like some of the girls in my class in Romania. I thought she was nice.

Next to each bed stood a small closet for personal belongings like books, notebooks, the week's supply of clothing, and anything else that was private, like a diary or an album. Ruti helped me to arrange my things. She warned me not to leave a diary lying around, because everyone would read it, Leah too.

I didn't have a diary. I did have my bag full of dolls, though, which was still at Miriam's, and I asked her if I could leave it there.

"All right," she said.

"Miriam," I said, "I promised my mother I'd write her as soon as I got here. She gave me an envelope with an address."

The envelope was a little wrinkled. Miriam gave the address a surprised look.

"Your mother is in Turkey? But this isn't your last name. Whose address is it?"

"My mother is in Romania, but she said she would get the letter more quickly if I sent it care of this address."

"I'll bring it to the office tomorrow and see that it's mailed. Here, sit down and write."

She gave me a pencil and paper and I wrote:

Dear Mama,

    I'm at the kibbutz. I'm in fifth grade. I live with three girls. We have a housemother and a class teacher and some other teachers. And lots of sun. And I have a "parent" too. Her name is Comrade Miriam. Don't worry. I can't wait for you to come! Bring Grandma. Love and xxxxx,

Lydia

I sealed the envelope and copied my Hebrew return address, which Miriam wrote for me on a piece of paper. "Palestine" and "Lydia" were already words I could write by myself.

CHAPTER NINE

Friends and Foes

O N MY FIRST FRIDAY at the kibbutz I went with my classmates for my weekly clothes bundle. Leah had prepared the bundles, each wrapped in a towel. In each was some underwear, a set of work clothes, and a set of regular clothes, besides which I was given a pair of brown work boots. We also received clothes for the Sabbath: blue skirts and white blouses for the girls, and blue pants and white shirts for the boys. I liked them the best. The dirty clothes that we brought back were sent to the laundry.

When I went through my bundle, I saw that none of my own clothes were in it, not even my underwear. The underwear was the only part that annoyed me, because I had much nicer panties than the kibbutz's. My other clothes didn't matter to me, since I wouldn't have worn them anyway. They were simply too different from what the kibbutz children wore. But I did want to have the beautiful dress my grandmother had made for my trip, even if it just hung in Miriam's closet.

We took our bundles back to the dorm and Leah came to make sure we all showered. During the week we washed at the sink, because the showers had no hot water and the weather was still cool. But on Fridays the water was heated and we all showered and washed our hair. The only part I minded was that the boys and girls had to shower together.

That was too much for me. "When do we start showering separately?" I asked.

"In sixth grade."

Just then I saw Leah say something to Ofra, who turned and left.

"Where's she going?" I asked Ruti.

"Leah sends her every Friday to clean her grandmother's room."

"If *she's* not showering with the boys," I said, "I'm not either."

I told Leah. "You'll shower like everyone else," she said grimly.

"What about Ofra?"

That made her so mad that she grabbed me without another word and began dragging me to the shower. She should have known better. I hung on to the door and started to scream. When she couldn't pry me loose, she decided to undress me. I was furious and started pulling at her own dress until it ripped. The children were too aghast to laugh. In the end I went without a shower and was summoned for a private talk with David before supper. Miriam and Dina were there also, and of course, Leah, too. I smiled to myself when I saw she had another dress on.

"You've gone too far," said David.

"No one can make me take my clothes off and shower with boys, not even Leah."

"She was just trying to reason with you. You shouldn't have attacked her and ripped her dress."

"Leah's a liar," I said. "Do you honestly think I jumped on her and ripped her dress for saying to me nicely, 'Lydia, would you like to take a shower?' Don't you know she tried pulling off my clothes? Ask the others. And while you're at it, why don't you ask her where she sends Ofra every Friday when everyone else is in the shower."

I was told I could go. From then on, the girls showered before the boys. I was proud of my victory, but Leah was now my enemy even without a declaration.

A few weeks went by. Every Friday Leah made sure to put the ugliest clothes in my bundle. The ones she gave me were also too small, so that I had to keep going back and changing them. One shirt I kept getting despite all my protests was so awful that I threw it in the garbage. Leah noticed it was missing and asked about it.

"I returned it to the laundry," I said innocently.

It was too bad I couldn't throw *her* in the garbage.

I decided to take my dolls out of their bag and hold an official ceremony. I tried thinking of ways to get the kibbutz to change Leah's job, but I couldn't come up with a plan. Maybe I should ask Ruti, I thought. When the children went to their parents' after school that day, I ran to Miriam's and opened the closet. My bag of dolls was gone.

"Miriam, where's the bag I put here?"

"What bag, Lydia?"

"The one I asked you to keep for me."

"Oh, the one with the dolls? I gave them away to the nursery. I forgot to tell you about it. I thought you were too big for them. Why, don't tell me you're crying!"

I hadn't wanted to, but I couldn't help it.

"I'll get them back for you," she said.

"Now! I want you to get them right now!"

"All right. You'll have to come with me, because I won't know which they are. They looked so junky . . . Well, never mind. Come along."

They did *not* look junky. They had nicer clothes than she did. But I was too upset to talk back. All I wanted was for her to get her shoes on and come with me. It took a while, because she was too fat to bend over easily.

We didn't find all the dolls. The housemother at the nursery said that one had been torn and thrown out, and that another had been lost in the yard. Maybe a dog had walked off with it. We found three dolls in the two- and three-year-olds' room and four more in the four- and five-year-olds' room. That Woman wasn't one of them. She had been my mother's favorite.

We took the dolls we found back to Miriam's room. I didn't want to play any of the usual games I played with her when I came back from school. I put my dolls in a corner and just sat there staring at them.

"I'll do anything to make up for it," said Miriam. "I can't tell you how sorry I am."

She felt awful, but I wasn't the least bit sorry for her. I was only sorry for my dolls. All I could think of was what they had been through. I didn't answer when she spoke to me. Anyone who could do such a thing was as big an enemy as Leah. She didn't get the point even now. I wouldn't come to her room anymore.

After school the next day, I went with Ruti to her parents'. When her mother asked me if Miriam wasn't in, I simply said, "Yes," which could have meant anything. I didn't mean to be unclear, it just came out that way.

Ruti's parents were very nice. They were so young that they seemed like children playing house, and Ruti's baby brother was adorable. When all the parents walked their children back to the dorm that evening, Miriam was waiting for me. She saw me walk up with Ruti and her parents.

"Lydia," she said, "where were you? I looked everywhere for you. I was worried something had happened."

"Nothing happened," I said.

She gave Ruti's mother a questioning glance.

"I'm really sorry," said Ruti's mother hesitantly. "Lydia told us that . . . that you weren't in."

I decided to take matters into my own hands and said loudly, "I didn't come because I didn't want to."

For a long time no one said a word. Then Ruti's father murmured, "We're very sorry. We didn't know."

"Lydia," said Miriam, turning to me, "I want to have a talk with you tomorrow afternoon."

"All right," I said.

I had to go back there for my dolls anyway.

The next day was a Friday. Miriam greeted me with a sour face and could hardly get a word out. She sounded as if she were talking from her grave. "Hello, Lydia. You really did humiliate me yesterday."

What could I say?

"You might at least say hello."

I was thinking so hard that I hadn't noticed that I didn't. "Hello," I said. "I came for my dolls."

"Where are you taking them?"

"To Ruti's parents."

"It's Friday. Every family sits together at the Sabbath dinner tonight."

"I'll sit with Ruti."

"All because of the dolls? I'll buy you a new doll. We'll go to a toy store in town. Wouldn't you like that? I really am sorry."

She didn't know I couldn't be bribed.

"I don't want to come here anymore."

"You have to. I was chosen to be your foster parent, don't you understand?"

"I don't have to do anything for anyone except my mother."

"But she's not here."

"Never mind, she will be."

I took my dolls and left. I don't remember if I said goodbye. I brought the bag to Ruti's parents and asked if I could leave it with them. "And I want to sit with you in the dining room," I said.

"Are these your private things that were at Miriam's?" Ruti's mother asked.

"Yes," I said.

"Has Miriam agreed to all this?" asked Ruti's father.

"No, she hasn't. I just told her I wasn't coming back."

"I suppose you can come with us this once," said Ruti's father after thinking a little. "But we'll have to talk it over with Dina. Miriam is supposed to be your foster parent until your mother comes."

"Well, she's fired," I said. They tried to hide their laughter, but I saw it.

The talk with Dina took place in her room on Sunday. I was afraid that everyone would be there, but there were only the two of us. Dina told me that Miriam had lodged a complaint that Ruti's parents had "kidnapped" me. I told her that I didn't want to go to Miriam's. No one could make me.

"Miriam told me what happened with the dolls. She didn't mean any harm. She's ready to apologize. She offered to buy you a new doll."

"It's not that," I said. "I just don't like her anymore."

"You should feel sorry for her," Dina said. "She's all alone here without family."

"But I want to go to Ruti's parents."

"Suppose they don't agree?"

"Why shouldn't they? They wouldn't only if you told them not to."

"What would you do then?"

"I wouldn't go anywhere."

Dina thought for a minute and said that she would talk to Miriam and that I could go wherever I liked.

I didn't go to Miriam's anymore. It was strange that someone as un-nice as Dina should be so nice to me.

I must say that at first I felt awful when I ran into Miriam in the dining hall or anywhere at the kibbutz. As soon as I spotted her I looked away and pretended not to see her. She wasn't an enemy like Leah to whom I would have wanted something bad to happen, but I couldn't stand her being near me or talking to me, even if I pitied her.

On the other hand, I liked to bump into Dina. My first class every morning was with her, which made it easier to get out of bed. I never came late, even in cold weather, when we all shivered on our way to the athletic field for our morning exercises. The coldest were the boys, who tried showing off by coming in their T-shirts, and Rina from the next room, who wore shorts even though her legs turned blue.

Every afternoon except Friday I had a private Hebrew lesson with Dina in her room from three to four. The first time in my life that I regretted my gift for languages was when she told me one day that my Hebrew was now good enough for her to stop tutoring me.

Dina had her own electric kettle — she was the only person at the kibbutz who did — and treated me to tea and cookies after each lesson. The cookies were the kind that melted in your mouth if you dunked them in the tea first, although of course you had to know how long to do it. If you didn't dunk them enough they stayed hard, while if you dunked them too much they crumbled and turned the tea into mud.

"You look tragic," said Dina. She liked to use nice words like that. "Is it because you're already missing your tea and cookies?"

I didn't answer.

She studied me and said, "Well, how would you like to be my guest for tea every Saturday afternoon? Just don't forget to tell Ruti's parents not to expect you then."

I wanted to hug her, but it wasn't the sort of thing you did, so I just said, "Oh, thank you, Dina," and ran like crazy back to the dorm.

Sometimes running like crazy helps.

❄❄❄❄❄❄❄

Dina's kettle was one of two private possessions at the kibbutz that were envied by everyone. The other was the radio received by Zalman as a present from the Jewish Brigade after he was wounded in the fighting in Europe.

Zalman lived in a shack at a far end of the kibbutz. One day I was sitting with Ruti on the front steps of our room when all of a sudden we heard music. We went to see where it was coming from and came running back to tell the children, "Come quick, Zalman has a radio!"

No one believed us, but everyone came anyway. And Zalman really did have a radio.

The only other radio at the kibbutz stood in a corner of the dining hall, and only the grownups were allowed to sit around it every evening while they read the newspaper and had bread and jam with tea. We children were always shooed away. So from the day we discovered Zalman's radio, we went to sit and listen beneath his window. "Zalman!" we would shout. "How about some Russian music?" A minute later we would hear a crackle of static that told us he was searching for a Russian station on his short-wave band, and after a while he would find it.

One day we arrived to find his room silent.

"Zalman! How about some Russian music?"

Zalman leaned out the window and informed us that his radio had been confiscated. There would be no more Russian songs.

We returned dejectedly to our dorm. I really felt for him. It was exactly the same as when my dress was taken away. *Suppose*, I thought, *they take Dina's kettle too?*

"It was Zalman's radio!" I said angrily.

"Maybe so, but there's no private property on the kibbutz," said Ofra with the pitying look that was reserved for city folk.

It ended happily, though, at least for us children, because at a kibbutz meeting they decided to put the radio in our reading room. Our joy knew no bounds. If anyone wanted music, he would say to the radio operator, "Zalman! How about some Russian songs?" There would follow the familiar crackle of static until a station was found. And every Friday, when it was someone else's turn to be in charge, we said to him, "All right, you're Zalman this week."

One day a theater director came to our school and held tryouts for a big performance that was going to be put on for the kibbutz's twentieth anniversary. Naturally, I was given a part. It helped to make up for losing the lead in my school play in Bucharest. Although it wasn't as big a part, it was a pretty good one. The only problem was my Romanian accent. Whenever I said my lines some of the girls started to giggle, especially Ada and Penina, and the next day in school they imitated me. I swore that I would learn to talk just the way they did, and I made Ruti sit down with me and correct all the words I said wrong.

Ruti was my best friend ever. It annoyed me that we weren't roommates.

"Let's think of a way to make them move you to my room," I said to her one day.

She didn't think it was possible. "Who would change with me? Ada and Penina are best friends, and Ofra will never agree."

"Then we'll have to make her."

We came up with all kinds of plans for making Ofra feel unwanted and decided to start with one of the simplest. Ruti wasn't afraid of animals, so she caught a toad and we put it in Ofra's bed when no one was looking. At first it crawled out, but we put it back and tucked it in so tight it couldn't escape. That night Ofra put on her pajamas, pulled back the blanket, and slipped into bed. A moment later she let out a loud screech and jumped out. The girls from the other room came running, and so did the boys.

Ruti played innocent and asked, "Ofra, what's wrong?"

Just then Leah came to turn out the lights. "Ma," Ofra cried, "there's something cold and wet in my bed!"

Leah lifted the blanket and the toad jumped out. We all burst out laughing except for her and Ofra, and in the end one of the boys grabbed the toad and everyone left the room. Leah gave Ofra a fresh sheet and pillowcase and we got back into bed.

When the lights were turned out in the other rooms, Leah came back and asked, "All right, who did it?"

No one spoke. Usually I own up, but this time I decided not to.

"Lydia, did you put that frog in Ofra's bed?"

"No," I lied.

It really went against the grain. But I wanted Ofra out of our room and couldn't think of any other way to do it. I couldn't resist adding, "It wasn't a frog. It was a toad."

"When I catch the little stinker who did it," said Leah in a fury, "I'll give her something to remember me by." She looked right at me as she said it, turned out the lights, and left without saying good night.

After a while I heard sobs. They came from Ofra's bed. I suddenly felt sorry for what I had done.

"Ofra?"

Ofra didn't answer. I got out of my bed and went to sit on hers.

"I put the toad in your bed. I'm sorry."

"Why did you do it? It's not my fault that my mother is the housemother."

"That wasn't why. I just wanted . . . You see, I wanted to room with Ruti. I thought that if we picked on you, you'd agree to move."

"But I don't mind changing with Ruti at all," said Ofra.

106

"I used to like this room because there were only three of us and it was less crowded. Now it doesn't make any difference. You only had to ask. But you all hate me because of my mother!"

"Ofra, I apologize. Are you really ready to change rooms?"

"I just told you I was."

"Do you think your mother will agree?"

"Yes."

The next day Ofra and Ruti changed rooms. Leah was a little taken aback, but she didn't interfere. And after that we stopped hating Ofra. It really wasn't her fault that her mother was the housemother.

CHAPTER TEN

❧❀❧

The English Teacher

EXCEPT FOR LEAH, I had no problems with the grown-ups. I liked Dina, and David was a good teacher, too. I also got along well with the gym teacher, maybe because I was the best broad jumper. But most of all, I loved Hannah, the English teacher.

Of course, I already knew more English than the other children because of Mister Lupo, and at first I was bored in class and made a pest of myself. Whenever Hannah said something to me I made some wisecrack back, until one day she asked me to stay after class.

"I'd like a word with you," she said in English.

I thought she didn't know any Hebrew. Later I found out that she did but wouldn't speak it to her pupils. She spoke English to me now, too, in simple words and sentences. Close up, I saw that she had bright, sky-blue eyes and wrinkles at her throat. She thought I was a city child who was being boarded in the kibbutz, and she gave me a long look when I told her that my mother was in Romania but would be coming soon. She didn't ask about my father.

"My mother has to get to Turkey," I explained. "Maybe the English will let her in from there."

"I'm English myself," said Hannah with a sigh.

"Then how come you have a Hebrew name?"

She told me that her real name was Ann and that she wasn't Jewish.

"Then why . . . " But I didn't finish my question, because it occurred to me that it might be impolite to ask why the English did not let Jews into Palestine, or what she was doing in the country — especially since I was there for a reprimand.

Hannah, however, seemed to have forgotten all about scolding me and began to explain what had brought her to Palestine. Although I didn't understand all she said, I gathered that her husband was an officer in the British army and that she hadn't wanted to stay behind in London. She had always been interested in Jews and the Holy Land, and especially in kibbutz life, which was why she had volunteered to teach us English.

"Without money?" I asked, to make sure I understood what "volunteered" meant.

"Without money."

Although I wanted to ask if she had children, I restrained myself again and asked what her husband did.

"He's an officer in the British army. I already told you, but perhaps you didn't understand."

"No, I did," I said. "I meant what does he *do* in the army."

109

"My husband is in such a special unit that I'm not sure myself what he does. He's not often at home and we have no children, which is why I enjoy coming here to teach. I like my work. Even," she said, smiling, "if sometimes a child gets cheeky."

There was a pause, and I was about to excuse myself when she asked, "And where on the kibbutz do you work?"

I told her about the nature corner and how I liked to feed the animals and didn't even mind cleaning the pens and cages.

"Do you miss your mother?"

"Sometimes. Sometimes I miss her very much. Especially when I've had a fight with someone. But sometimes I forget that I'm here all by myself."

"I miss my parents in London terribly. I'm worried about them, too."

"You have parents in London?"

"Yes. They're very old. And very nice."

I would never had imagined that grownups like Hannah had parents somewhere too.

"Why are you worried?"

"Because of the German air raids. You may not know it, but the Germans bomb London all the time."

I really hadn't known.

From that day on, I couldn't wait for our English lessons. Hannah made me her assistant and after class I would walk her to the teachers' room. We had English on Sundays and Wednesdays. The Sunday lesson was right before recess, and since the teachers' room was near our classroom, she and I would stand halfway between the two rooms and chat. The Wednesday lesson was the day's last, and after it I would walk Hannah to the bus stop and wait with her for the bus. We had lots of time then to talk, so I told her all my stories about Romania — about our trips to the mountains, vacations with Mihai and Ion, my governesses, Marioara, Mister Lupo and how I got rid of him, and Adriana who always ran to her mother. I told her about my dolls too, and about the weddings and funerals that I had for them, and about declaring someone an enemy.

"You know," she said, "there are tribes in Africa and other faraway places that do the same thing when they want to kill or win a war against their enemies. There's even a ceremony called 'voodoo' in which you take a doll that represents the enemy and pretend to kill it. That means your enemy will die, too."

"And does he?"

"I don't know." She laughed. I didn't really want to kill Leah.

Another time Hannah asked me if I liked school. I had never asked myself that question before.

"Yes," I said after thinking about it.

"I do believe that the children here are quite happy. I wish I had gone to a school like yours when I was a child."

Hannah told me about the boarding school she had gone to. She told me what the girls wore to class and to afternoon tea, to church on Sunday and to dances with the boys from a nearby school. She hadn't liked it there.

111

"Then why didn't you run away?" I asked.

"With my upbringing I never would have thought of such a thing."

We talked until the bus came, and she always waved to me from the window.

One Wednesday I noticed that Ruti gave me a dirty look when I came back from the bus stop.

"Ruti, what's wrong?"

"Where were you?"

"What's the matter? I walked Hannah to the bus."

"You follow her around like a leech. It's disgusting."

"If it's disgusting, don't look. What do you want from me?"

"She's old enough to be your mother. All she has to do is smile and you get dewy-eyed."

"You're just jealous!"

"I am not! You can be friends with whoever you like." Ruti turned and walked off.

We didn't talk to each other for the rest of the day. I didn't go to her parents' either.

That evening her mother asked me where I had been. "Ruti said you couldn't come."

"Yes," I said. "A goat gave birth in the nature corner. I wanted to see it."

A goat really had given birth, but that was two days earlier.

In our beds that night we ignored each other and pretended to read until Leah turned out the lights.

The next day in school there was a transparent wall between us. And this time, when I saw her mother in the evening, she didn't ask where I had been. I felt so hurt that I even thought of looking for new "parents."

During recess the next day, however, Ruti came over to me and said, "I want to talk to you."

That made me feel better instantly, even though I had no idea what she was going to say.

"My mother says it's all right for a boy or girl our age to have a grown-up friend, especially if they have no family of their own."

"Who told you to tell your mother?" I asked angrily. I didn't want her to act like Adriana.

"I didn't mean to. She saw me crying."

"Why were you crying?"

"Don't be a dope," said Ruti. "I was crying because of you."

CHAPTER ELEVEN

❧❦❧

The Straw that Broke the Camel's Back

I DON'T REMEMBER what I had stepped out for when suddenly I saw Ofra on her way to the bus station in my dress. She was with her mother. I knew they were going to visit relatives in Tel Aviv, but no one had told me that she was going to wear my "city dress." Although I was sure she didn't even know it was mine, seeing it on her made me feel blue.

I went to the teachers' room and asked to talk to David about a private matter. He told me to come back during recess, and when I did he took me outside. There I told him that my father was a journalist who had left Romania for Palestine at the beginning of the war to work for an English newspaper. I said that I wanted to look for him.

"What made you decide to do that now?"

"I miss him," I said.

David knew I had a vivid imagination and he was skeptical, so I went to Ruti's parents and brought back the photograph of my parents and the letter my father had written on the Red Cross form. This time he was dumbfounded.

"But why didn't you ask us to look for him before?"

"My mother told me not to."

For a moment neither of us spoke. He looked at me curiously. "And now she's changed her mind?"

"I don't know. She promised to come and she hasn't."

For a while he seemed lost in thought. "When did your father arrive in this country?"

"A few months before his letter came."

He looked at the letter again. "Why didn't he take you with him?"

"He had to leave Romania in a hurry, because he worked for an English paper and there was a Fascist pogrom and Jews were hung alive on butcher hooks."

"That's ridiculous, Lydia. You should be ashamed of yourself."

"It is *not* ridiculous. It's what happened. In the end they were taken down and buried."

"But why didn't you come with him?"

"Because of Rommel. My father didn't want him to catch us here."

"Why wasn't he afraid of Rommel, too?"

"He was more afraid of the Iron Guard."

That same afternoon we went to the kibbutz office, and the secretary promised to place an ad on the radio.

"Is there an English newspaper here?" I asked. "If there is, he probably reads it."

"An ad in the paper would be very expensive."

"He'll pay you back."

I told Ruti about it. I didn't want her to have to hear from someone else.

She asked in alarm, "And if you find him . . . you'll leave us?"

I was alarmed by that too.

"No, I could never do that. My mother will come looking for me here."

"But suppose she . . . "

"Well, I can always stay on as a boarding student."

That reassured her.

By the time Ruti's parents arrived, they had already heard all about it. They too wanted to know why my father had come to Palestine without us, and why my mother hadn't wanted me to look for him.

"She said she'd explain it all when she got here," I said.

They looked at each other and asked no more questions. That evening Ruti told me what she had overheard them saying to each other.

"They think your parents must have quarreled, and that maybe they're even divorced."

"That's impossible," I said.

My parents divorced? I couldn't imagine anything more awful. I would rather one of them died. That at least was nothing to be ashamed of.

"Do you know anyone whose parents are divorced?" I asked Ruti.

She thought for a while. "When I was little, there was someone who had to leave the kibbutz because he divorced his wife and wanted to marry Penina's mother. As a matter of fact, you know the woman he divorced. It's Miriam."

"I didn't know she was married."

"She was. She just never talks about it."

I made Ruti swear never to tell anyone, not even her parents, and after she had sworn to God and said, "Hope to die," I told her about That Woman, my father's mistress from Dudeşti.

"I'll find him," I told her. "And if he's still with her, I'll find a way to get rid of her."

"How?"

"I don't know yet, but you can count on me."

One Wednesday when I walked Hannah to the bus, she said that she had heard about my father and asked if that was the reason I looked sad. Although I hadn't known I did, I could feel the sadness in my face the minute she said it. I told her it was.

"Do you know why your father came without you?"

"It was because of the war. But afterwards he sent a certificate to That Woman. No one on the kibbutz knows about her except Ruti, and she swore not to tell."

"And it's because of her that your mother didn't want you to look for him?"

"Yes. She said that she would find him when she came."

"Did she say that he had married her?"

"Of course not! How could he marry her if he and my mother aren't divorced?"

"Do you know her?"

"No. I've never even seen her. All I know is that her name is Lili."

117

"I see," said Hannah. She thought for a while and said, "Lydia, if your father is still in Palestine and has any contact with the British, my husband can track him down. I promise you that. But you have to realize that you may be disappointed. Who knows if you'll be able to live with him, or if you'll even want to?"

"But I don't. I'm waiting for my mother. I just want to find him. My mother promised to come but she hasn't."

Two weeks later Hannah and her husband brought my father to the kibbutz. I was called out of an arithmetic class by Hanan, the the kibbutz secretary. He walked with me to the front gate.

In the distance I saw a square, black car, and next to it a man in a suit. I began to run then threw myself into his arms, and he picked me up and swung me high in the air as he used to do when I was little. I didn't cry, although I thought I was going to. He hadn't changed. He was the same father I remembered and he even still wore his city clothes.

"Papa! Just look at how you're dressed!"

I hadn't meant that to be the first thing I said after not seeing him for so long, but it was what came out.

"Would you rather I dressed like a kibbutznik?" he asked with a smile.

"No!" I said after a second.

The doors of the car opened and out stepped my English teacher and a British officer who was as tall as my father. I shook Hannah's hand and then I shook her husband's. Hanan did, too, although shaking hands was not a kibbutz custom.

"Can I take her home with me until Sunday?" asked my father.

"Of course," said Hanan. "But first I'd like to talk to you for a minute. Why don't you come to the office? Lydia will show you where it is."

"I'm afraid I can't stay very long," said my father, "because I don't want to keep the major and his wife waiting. I'm sure Lydia will want to get a few things, and we can talk here while she's doing it."

The two of them walked behind the car and began to converse in low voices.

"You see," said Hannah, "we found him!"

That's when I did something I had never done for anyone before: I stepped up to the major and told him in English that I wanted to thank him for helping me.

"It was my pleasure, Lydia," he said. "Ann has told me so much about you."

Hanan waved goodbye and went off.

My father said to me, "Hanan told me that your housemother is waiting to give you some things. Let's get a move on. I don't want to hold up your friends."

I put my hand in his and we walked together. What did I care that girls my age in the kibbutz didn't hold hands with their fathers? It gave me a good feeling.

After a few steps he asked, "Lydia, what are you doing here? How did you get here?"

That was how our meeting should have started. I told him.

"But why didn't your mother write me?"

"Papa, you never sent us your address. You wrote us

exactly one letter on a Red Cross form and the only return address was 'Jerusalem.' "

"That's right. I didn't give you an address then because I didn't have one yet. But afterwards I wrote you two or three more letters that did have my return address on them."

"We never got them."

"I also asked someone who was going to Romania to get in touch with you, but he said you weren't in the apartment."

"We moved."

"How is Mama?"

"Fine. And you?"

Just then Leah came and we had to stop talking. She couldn't have been nicer and was sweet as sugar to my father. All witches are like that.

"Hanan said that you're going away for a few days," she said to me. "I've prepared a bag of things for you. Come with me to the storeroom, please. Is there anything else you need?"

"No," I said, "I don't need anything. I'd just like to have my dress."

"Your dress? Oh, yes. Come, I'll give it to you."

We went to the storeroom. Leah opened the closet, which was full of all the city clothes that we never wore on the kibbutz. My dress was hanging there. She took it and gave it to me.

"You can put it on here," she said.

"No, I'll put it on in my room."

"Here's your bag," said Leah. "Have a good trip." She

turned to my father and said, "It was nice meeting you."

"Likewise," said my father.

You would never have guessed she was the same person.

We went to my room. My father was curious to see the whole dorm, so I took him to the other rooms first. He sat on my bed while I showed him my chest of drawers and Ruti's bed. "This is where my best friend sleeps." I should have said goodbye to her when I ran from the classroom, but I was sure she would understand.

He looked at the pictures on the walls, some of which were hung by Leah and some by us. Ruti's father had hammered in the nails for us. On the chest by each bed was a napkin with a little vase of flowers. "I'll bet the rooms without flowers and napkins belong to the boys," my father said.

"You're right." I laughed.

I asked him to wait in the next room while I put on the dress. Suddenly I felt embarrassed. He had become a bit of a stranger to me after all.

The dress was small on me. I had suspected it would be as soon as I took it from the storeroom. I could see Leah measure both it and me with her eyes and purse her lips, although she didn't say anything. She wanted me to find out for myself. I wasn't sure if that made me think more or less of her.

I stuck the dress in my bag. I didn't care if it fit me or not. The kibbutz wasn't going to have it.

"Lydia," said my father, "sit down. I have to talk to you."

Before I could, there were footsteps and in came Dina.

121

All of a sudden I was a big attraction. I introduced her to my father. They shook hands and she said, "You have a wonderful daughter. She's as bright and talented as they come. And in case you don't know . . . prepare yourself, because she likes to have her own way. We've discovered that she's quite an actress, too. She's in a play we're putting on for the kibbutz's twentieth anniversary and you're invited — if, that is, you intend to let her remain with us."

"We haven't had a chance to talk about any of that yet," said my father, "but we have until Sunday to make a decision. Right now we're going to town."

"I'll walk you to the car," said Dina.

My father took my bag and we returned to the car. Hannah introduced Dina to her husband and they talked politely in English, exchanging the same phrases that were in our grammar book. It was funny to hear those model conversations, which had never seemed real to me, actually being spoken.

Just as we got into the car, I heard someone shouting my name. It was Ruti, who was running across the forbidden lawn to take a shortcut. "Lydia, wait!" she cried.

How could I have been so stupid as to forget to say goodbye to her? It all came from being so excited.

"Are you going?"

"Just till Sunday."

"Whew, I was scared! You didn't even say goodbye."

"I know. It was awful of me. There was just so much . . . going on." I didn't want to say "excitement." "But I'm so glad you came. Here, this is my father."

My father held his hand out through the window. Ruti was startled, but she shook it.

" 'Bye!" I said.

I leaned against my father and he put his arm around me. The car pulled out of the kibbutz. I wanted to ask if he was living with That Woman and how many rooms he had, but I couldn't talk about those things in English and it wasn't polite to do it in Romanian. We drove in silence for a while until I asked how my father had been found. Hannah explained that it was through some secret work that he did for the British. Even her husband didn't know exactly what it was.

"What do you do?" I asked him.

It was funny speaking English to him, although in fact he spoke it very well.

"I work in what's called 'psychological warfare.' That means I broadcast over the radio in Romanian. I try to convince the Romanian people to overthrow the Fascists and resist the German war effort, if you know what that means."

"War effort? I guess that's all the things you do to fight a war. Do you really talk on the radio?"

"Yes, but it's not an ordinary radio," said my father. "I mean, it sounds like an ordinary radio in Romania, but it has a frequency that not everyone knows."

"Do you work in Jerusalem?"

I knew that all the radio stations were there.

"No. We make believe we're broadcasting from Syria, but we're actually somewhere else. It's a secret place.

Traveling back and forth takes a lot of time, and Lili is always complaining."

The conversation stopped. So he still lived with Lili! I could feel my face burn.

After a while Hannah began to talk to my father about Palestine. Then her husband interrupted and asked me about my school. He spoke slowly and chose easy words so that I could understand all his questions, though now and then an expression was beyond me.

"Did you learn your English here?" he asked.

"Yes and no," I said. "I knew a little before I came, because I took lessons from a man in Bucharest."

"A man in Bucharest?" asked my father.

"Yes. He came to give Mama and me lessons. Mama thought we might go to America. She thought English would be good to know in Palestine, too."

"Who was this man?" my father asked.

"An actor I knew. The Fascists broke his leg and he couldn't work, so Mama gave him meals for English lessons. You know, we sold all your books. And lots of other things too."

My father wanted to hear more about Mister Lupo. "Since when were your friends actors?"

I told him the whole story. I just left out the part about the kisses Mister Lupo had given my mother. There was silence again, and then Hannah's husband asked me about Bucharest and the Fascists. He didn't seem to think I was making it up when I told him about the butcher shop. I also told him what I had heard about the Jews in Bessarabia and Bukovina after the Romanians captured them from the Russians.

I didn't notice that we were already in a city.

"You can let us off here," said my father.

We thanked them, shook hands again, and climbed out of the car. We were standing on a side street by the entrance to a large apartment house. On the corner was a little café. It was a perfect place for my father to live, I thought, because I could make him buy me all kinds of good things there. But first I had some business to take care of.

"Come on," he said.

I didn't. I just took a deep breath.

"What's the matter?"

That's when I started to scream. I yelled, "Get that yucky woman out of the house! You sent her a certificate for Palestine and left Mama and me in Romania! Get her out and send Mama a certificate!"

"But Lydia . . . " he began to mumble confusedly. "I . . . stop screaming!"

"I will not!" I shouted, taking a few steps back for safety's sake. "Will everybody on this street please listen to the kind of neighbor you have! He left me and my mother in Romania and sent our certificate to his mistress! I'm talking about that yucky moron from Dudeşti! Listen, all of you: it's time you realize who this man is! And it's time the thief who stole my father realizes too and clears out!"

I don't know how this whole speech gave itself as if I had prepared it in advance, because I had no idea a second beforehand what I was going to do. All at once everything seemed so clear that I didn't have to think twice. The words came out by themselves, like a part in a play that I'd learned by heart — and the more I screamed, the more I felt like screaming. My mother would have called it "acting out."

The whole time, I kept eyeing the windows to see if the neighbors were listening. In fact, the windows began filling with spectators, most of them children, but some of them grown men and women. I was afraid to stop for breath, because I knew that my father would grab me and put an end to it. He actually did try catching and gagging me, but he had forgotten that I was stronger than the little girl he remembered, and I escaped and went on screaming while dodging behind some bushes. He ran after me on his long legs and caught me again, this time more forcefully, shaking me hard while covering my mouth. I threw myself on the ground and kicked wildly, and the minute he let go of me I jumped up and dashed into the house.

Just then a man came outside and grabbed hold of him. "What are you doing to that girl? I'll call the police!"

"She's my daughter," said my father in a fury. "We're having a family problem. I'll thank you to keep out of it."

A family problem? So that's what it was called! Although I didn't know what floor he lived on, it hardly mattered anymore. If That Woman was anywhere in the building, she would have heard me by now, and if she wasn't, she would hear from the neighbors.

126

The man let go of Papa and ran after me. "Is he really your father?" he asked.

"Of course he's my father!" I screamed loud enough for the whole building to hear. "That's what I keep telling you! He sent this woman he's living with a certificate to Palestine and left me and my mother behind . . . "

My father grabbed me again and this time I stood no chance. I thrashed my arms and legs while he picked me up under his arm and ran with me as though I were a package, scooping up my bag on the way and boarding a bus with me. I hadn't even seen the bus standing there. I didn't say anything. Neither did he. The few passengers looked at us curiously, but my father had barely paid the driver when we got off at the first stop.

We were on a quiet street, with apartment buildings on both sides. Not far away was a small park with some benches. He dragged me to it and made me sit down on a bench.

"Ouch!" I screamed. "Let go of me!"

"Lydia," he said, "there's something I have to tell you."

I thought he was going to say something terrible, like that he and my mother were divorced and he was married to Lili. But it was nothing of the sort.

"That house you were screaming at is not where I live."

"It isn't?"

"No. No one there even knows me."

"Why didn't you say so?"

"I was trying my best."

All that screaming wasted, I thought. "Where do you live?"

He pointed to a house behind him.

"Honestly?"

"Honestly."

Our eyes met — and we burst out laughing. Or at least he did. I wasn't sure if I was laughing or crying.

"You really could be an actress. And what a voice!"

"Then why did we get out of the car there?" I asked, wiping my tears with my father's handkerchief.

"Because there's a little café on that street where I wanted to sit, buy you a treat, and have a talk. We have a lot to talk about."

I looked around me. There was nothing but houses, not even a corner kiosk. On top of everything, I had lost my chance for a piece of cake.

"What do we have to talk about?"

My father thought for a minute. "Let's start with the certificate," he said. "It's true that I sent one to Lili, but as soon as the Germans were driven back in North Africa I sent one to you, too. It came back with an 'Address Unknown' stamp. I was very worried and sent it again with the person I mentioned, but he couldn't find you either. You say you moved?"

"Lots of times."

"Then you understand what happened."

"I don't understand why you didn't send for us before the Germans were driven back."

He put his arm around me. "Lydia, I wasn't going to endanger you and your mother when it was safer to be in Romania. Lili is a grown woman without children. It's not the same thing."

"Where is she?"

"She's waiting for us at home."

I wriggled free from his arm and hugged my knees.

"If you promise me that you'll be nice to her, Lydia, I'll take you there now. If not, we can go back to the kibbutz. I don't want any encores of your performance."

"What does 'being nice' mean?"

"You don't have to fall all over her. I'm just asking you to be as polite as you would be anywhere, especially in someone's home. All right?"

I didn't have to fall all over her — what a way to put it! As a matter of fact, I would have loved to fall all over her and strangle her.

"Lydia," said my father, "if you're still spoiling for a fight, I'll take you back to the kibbutz. You can think it over, and if you change your mind you can write me and I'll come and bring you here again."

"And in the meantime?"

"I'll visit you there."

"By yourself?"

"In the meantime. How come Mama sent you all alone?"

"Because the man who's supposed to smuggle her to Turkey wouldn't take children. He'll take her in a fishing boat and then she'll come to the kibbutz."

"And you'll live with her there?"

"Yes."

"Did Mama give you instructions on what to do when you got here?"

"She told me to write her."

"Did you?"

"Yes."

"The Red Cross letters take a very long time, if they ever arrive at all."

"I wrote her to an address in Turkey."

"She didn't tell you to look for me?"

"No. She told me not to mention you in the kibbutz and said she would find you when she came. She promised to come soon."

"Your teacher says you've been here for half a year. What a misunderstanding! Your mother must have thought that . . . that I had forgotten about you. And I hadn't at all. Didn't she realize how much I love you?"

"But why did you bring That Woman?"

"That has nothing to do with it."

No one spoke until he asked, "Well, what now?"

"I'm hungry," I said.

"There's a good meal waiting for you. It's up to you."

At least he didn't say "Lili has cooked you a good meal" or "Lili is waiting for you."

"All right," I said. "I'll come and I'll be nice."

I was curious. More than just curious. Dying of curiosity! I prayed to God she would be ugly.

CHAPTER TWELVE

❦

I'm Devastated. She's Nice!

THE WORST PART of it was that she was pretty. She was even prettier than my mother. She was young, too, and had a good figure, though I never could see what was so good about being thin. When she opened the door, she gave me a big smile. Her teeth were all right too. My only consolation was her nostrils: one was bigger than the other. I hated uneven nostrils. Well, perhaps "hated" is a bit strong, but I never thought they looked nice. At least not until now . . .

She was dressed nicely also. Was that for my sake? For my father's? Maybe for both of us. I said hello, and she said, "Hello, Lydia. My, what a pretty girl you are!"

I almost made some comment, like "Who asked you?" or "Flattery will get you nowhere," but I didn't. Still, when she took my bag from my father, I couldn't control myself and snatched it back.

My father said, "Come, Lydia, let's put the bag in your room."

That Woman came with us.

A room of my own — that was a surprise! Of course, my grandmother would have sniffed and said, "Everything has a price." But if they thought they could buy me with my own room they were wrong. My father explained that they had moved his study into their bedroom and put a bed in the empty room for me. There were pictures on the walls, and there was even a clothes closet with a big mirror on the door.

That Woman went back to the kitchen. I breathed a sigh of relief and said to my father, "She dresses so awfully!"

"That's a matter of taste," he said. "If you ask me, she looks especially nice today."

"For my benefit?"

"No, for mine. And she has a nice perfume on, too."

"Yes," I said. "I noticed that stink."

"Lydia, you're not keeping your promise."

"I am too."

"You snatched your bag away from Lili."

"I *took* it."

"You're not fooling anyone. Just look at how you're talking."

"But I'm alone with you and she can't hear me."

"*I* don't want to hear you either. You can keep your thoughts to yourself."

I didn't answer, even though I'm used to getting in the last word. I went over to the closet.

"Is it empty?"

"Not entirely."

I opened the door.

"There's lots of room for your things," said my father. "We cleared two shelves for you, too."

So I had noticed. And speaking of being nice, he could have said "I" instead of "we."

"Who hung all the pictures?" I asked.

His only answer was, "They stay up. If you come here more often, you can hang whatever you like in their place."

It was too bad that because her name started with the same letter as mine, now I couldn't hang anything with an "L." I couldn't stand the way he said it either, in the same soft voice in which he sometimes said "Lydia."

"Lydia, you know I mean it. The minute you get out of line I'm packing your things and taking you back."

"All right, Papa."

I could see that I would have to change tactics.

I hung my dress in the closet and looked at the other things hanging there. I was glad to see that all were my father's.

That Woman began setting the table in the living room. "In your honor we'll eat out here," she said. "Our kitchen is tiny."

Their kitchen! I looked at her. She looked back. Her smile was gone. "Would you like something to drink, Lydia?" she asked.

All I wanted was for her to stop saying "Lydia." It was too bad she couldn't call me "Fraulein," or "Mademoiselle," or even "Comrade."

"No, thank you," I said in my most witchy-sweet voice.

"Come wash up," she said.

"I'll wash up with my father."

He went with me to the bathroom. "Lydia . . . "

"What is it now?" I snapped.

"Nothing," he said. "Just be civil, that's all."

And I was. I was so civil that I hoped it would give her bad dreams. I kept saying "please" and "thank you" in my most syrupy voice, even when there wasn't any need for it. One "thank you" in particular was so overdone that the two of them burst out laughing, and I even had to laugh myself. I couldn't hold it back. I can be as mad as anything, but the minute something funny happens I break into helpless giggles.

That Woman served tomato soup with rice. She must have asked my father what my favorite foods were, because I love tomato soup, especially with sour cream. Still, I was proud to hear myself say, "No, thank you. I used to like tomato soup, but I don't anymore. Especially not with rice and sour cream."

The problem was that they didn't insist. They simply took my plate away and that was that. I had to sit there watching them eat while my stomach growled. *Lydia*, I tried comforting myself, *you couldn't swallow anything That Woman makes anyway. Just one spoon of her soup and you'd throw up.*

"Can I have a slice of bread, please?" I asked.

"Of course, I'll get you one," she said, rising from her seat.

"No! I want my father to get it."

"I'll bring it," said my father.

134

Although I didn't think so then, I'm sure now that he knew how I felt. I kept eating more bread, because I wouldn't touch the breaded chicken breasts either. Or the french fries. Or the carrots and peas. At least that was something I really didn't like, because I preferred keeping my carrots and peas separate. But when the dessert came and That Woman brought bowls of ice cream with chocolate fudge, I gave in. I didn't think she had made the fudge herself, and to be on the safe side, I didn't ask. I wolfed it down and said "Yes, please" when I was asked if I wanted more.

I wanted it so badly that I even forgot to sound syrupy.

Next to each plate was a napkin in a silver holder. Maybe it was even real silver. When King Carol left Romania with his mistress and fifty railroad cars, he must have had gold napkin holders in one of them. I was still hungry. I wiped my mouth. The smells from the kitchen were driving me mad. If only they would stop!

My father said, "That was a wonderful meal, Lili dear. I really appreciate it."

He laid his hand on hers and stroked her cheek. That was really too much for me. I got up from the table so theatrically that I knocked over my chair, ran to my room, slammed the door, and threw myself on the bed. My father didn't come after me.

❈❈❈❈❈❈❈

I awoke in a fright. I didn't know where I was. Wondering, I looked at the window, through which shone a dim light that could have been dawn or dusk. Beyond it I could see an apartment house. Then I remembered.

It must have been late afternoon. I was covered with a light blanket, which someone had come in and put over me while I was asleep. I gave a start. Was it That Woman? I hoped it was my father. Whoever it was had taken my sandals off too, because I had been wearing them when I dozed off.

I rose, walked barefoot to the door, and opened it carefully. There was no one in the living room. The table was bare except for a fresh tablecloth and a vase of gladiolas. I hated gladiolas. I started for the bathroom, but a magnetic force made me change direction. The door to their bedroom was closed. I stood listening outside it for a minute, heard nothing, and let my feet take me to the kitchen.

The pots were still on the stove. I found a spoon and attacked the soup. Then I remembered the sour cream. From the sink I took a dirty bowl that no one would notice, and I started toward the refrigerator. Suppose she had eaten from it, though? I put it back in the sink, found the sour cream, stuck a gob of it in my mouth, and began eating the soup. But it didn't taste the way it should have, so I filled a clean bowl with soup, added more sour cream, and stirred. I liked watching the cream break up into stripes that drifted away in the soup.

The soup was really good, but so what? As long as I didn't say so, I wasn't a traitor. I took a second helping, washed and dried the bowl, and put it back in the closet with the clean dishes. Then I turned to the chicken breasts and french fries. I shoveled them up with my fingers and started in on the carrots and peas. That Woman had used a delicious spice that I couldn't make out, and I was still spooning the vegetables into my mouth from the pot when I heard a door open.

At first I froze. Then I put the spoon in the sink and slipped into the hallway. It was empty, but I didn't go back to the kitchen. I went to the bathroom, washed my hands and face, returned to my room, and lay down to read. I heard another door open and then my father knocked on mine.

"Come in," I said.

He did. "Are you up?"

"I just awoke."

"Lydia, I have to talk to you."

"Yes, Papa."

"You promised to be nice."

"I was nice."

"What kind of show were you putting on? You didn't eat a thing."

"I ate the ice cream."

"And that's all. To say nothing of your grand exit and knocking over your chair."

"I didn't do it on purpose."

"And the rest?"

"Don't you dare touch her when I'm around! And don't call her 'dear' either, do you hear me?"

My father sighed. He sat there thinking for a while,

then said in a friendly voice, "You know, Lydia, there's no point in talking about all this now. I thought we might go to a movie. Would you like that?"

"With her?"

"With her."

I wasn't going to let That Woman make me miss a movie. In the kibbutz we only had one movie a week, which was shown on the lawn and wasn't always for children. And this was a Charlie Chaplin, so I agreed. I even remember its name: *The Great Dictator*. I loved Chaplin even in Romania.

There were two empty seats on the bus. That Woman sat in one of them while my father stood and tried to get me to sit next to her, but I stood too. Naturally, I didn't sit between them in the movie either, the way I used to do in Romania when my parents took me to the circus or a show.

It was late when we got home. My father put me to bed. He wasn't finished when That Woman came into my room. She had no right to, but I didn't say anything. She smiled that pretty smile of hers — it was all right to think it as long as I didn't say it! — and said, "Good night, Lydia."

"Good night," I said sweetly.

I missed my mother. In the kibbutz the housemother would say "Good night, children" and turn out the lights, after which we would talk in whispers until we fell asleep. Here it was more like home, though. My father kissed me and tucked me in. He didn't cover me the same way I was covered that afternoon, which made me sure That

Woman had done it. By now I couldn't even feel angry. My father's kiss had stubbles of hair on it.

"Papa, I want to ask you a private question."

That Woman left the room. My father sat on the edge of my bed.

"Are the two of you married?"

"Yes. Didn't you realize that?"

"I didn't think you were yet."

He started to rise.

"How could you?"

He sat down again. "What do you mean, how could we? Didn't your mother tell you?"

I didn't say anything. I just stared at him and waited for the worst.

"Didn't she tell you we were divorced before I left?" he said.

I shook my head.

"Lydia, you know I'll always be your father. And Mama will always be your mother. No matter what."

I covered my head with the pillow.

"And Lili likes you very much."

"That's all you have to say to me? The last thing I need to hear now is how she likes me!"

"I'm sorry you only realized now. If I had known, I would have prepared you for it differently. It simply never occurred to me. I'm sorry, Lydia. It was a misunderstanding."

I kept silent.

"Good night, Lydia."

I heard him leave the room.

I woke up in the middle of the night, or perhaps it was early in the morning. In the dorm a light was always left burning in the hallway, but here it was pitch black, so I switched on the reading lamp over my bed and lay celebrating my victory. All alone in a room of my own, in which I could wake when I pleased and turn on the light when I wanted! Just then, though, I remembered that my parents were divorced. I switched off the light and lay in the dark.

I couldn't go back to sleep. I kept thinking about my parents and That Woman. I told myself, it's all over with. You haven't the ghost of a chance.

After a while I heard voices. I rose, went to the door, and opened it a crack. The bedroom door was open and they were talking. I heard Lili say that she would raise me to be a beautiful child, just as if I were her own daughter.

"Suppose her mother comes?"

"Suppose she does. But what about in the meantime? You know that I'm going to be thirty-two next week. I'm willing to wait one more year, and then I want a baby, war or no war."

My father didn't respond.

"What will we do about Lydia's food tomorrow?" she asked.

"I guess we'll have to eat sandwiches."

"All right. But only because this is her first time here. There's a limit."

"She knocked that chair over because I touched you."

"I know. You would think she'd been jilted by a lover."

What a creep, I thought. *Who does she think she is? He's not my lover, he's my father!*

She kept on talking. I could tell from what she said that my father had told her about my screaming in the street. I wasn't at all ashamed. What for? Let *her* be!

"Good for her!" I heard That Woman say. "I want you to know that you have a very special child. I'd love to know what will become of her. Is she like her mother?"

I shut the door quietly, though part of me wanted to hear what my father would say about my mother. Would it be nice or nasty? It was better not to know. I got back into bed and curled up under the blanket, which is something I need to do even in summer. She had no right to mention my mother. My father shouldn't discuss her. He had been in love with her once.

I turned the light back on and took from my bag a flat tin box that had a black cat's head on the lid. I opened it and undid my parents' wedding picture from the napkins in which it was wrapped. How could a man and a woman fall in love and marry, and then become such strangers that they could fall in love again with someone else?

Suppose they had a baby boy? Would he be my brother? I didn't know anyone that this had happened to. I missed my friends. Now that I was far away from her, I didn't even hate Leah so much.

In the morning I was awakened by my father.

"Lydia! Why don't you and I have a picnic today?"

"Just the two of us?"

"Lili has a headache. We'll be a twosome."

God was good! He should only give her headaches all

the time, one right after the other. I jumped out of bed. We ate breakfast together, then my father took a lunch basket that was already prepared and we left. Was I glad to be out of there!

"Papa, will the two of you have children?"

"Maybe after the war."

Well, I thought cheerfully, *the war may last a long time. Maybe it would never end. Rommel, come back to Africa!*

"Does that worry you?" he asked.

"Not right now," I said.

"Would you like to stay with us until Sunday?"

"Yes," I said. "Just tell her not to cook."

"Don't expect *me* to cook!"

"We can eat out."

"We have no money for restaurants. By the way, there were a whole lot of mice in the kitchen yesterday afternoon!"

He winked at me. I kept a straight face, but he knew that I had eaten her food.

My father found a nice wooded area with a stream and some other families with children. We spread out our blanket and I went to see what games the children were playing. I watched for a while then joined them and suggested we play king-of-the-mountain. They played it in the city too.

When I came back to my father a long while later, he was sleeping. He woke up when I sat down next to him and looked at his watch.

"My goodness, it's late! Are you hungry?"

I was. I didn't even ask who had made the sandwiches.

"I was glad to hear you have a big part in the play," he said.

"Will you come see it?"

"Of course. We both will."

He stole a glance at me. I said nothing, so he said, "By the way, if you like theater, I'm sure Lili will take you to one of her performances."

I sat up. "What?!"

"Lili performs in a soldiers' club. She's a singer. A very good one."

"I'm not too crazy about singers." That was all I needed. Still, I asked, "What does she sing?"

"All kinds of things. She has a song called 'Santa Lucia,' for instance. Have you ever heard of it?"

I nearly choked on my sandwich. When I managed to swallow, I said, "Papa, I want to go back to the kibbutz."

"You won't stay until Sunday?"

"No. I want to go back right now!"

CHAPTER THIRTEEN

❧

I Want to Wait for My Mother

W HEN I GOT BACK to the kibbutz, I didn't feel like talking about my visit with my father — not even to Ruti or her parents. After our Wednesday English lesson, though, I told Hannah all about it. This was the first time she didn't mind speaking with me in Hebrew.

"You should be glad that Lili is nice. Just imagine if she were mean," she said.

I hadn't thought of it that way. "But they're divorced!" I said.

"At least that's been settled."

"But my mother . . . "

"Your mother isn't here yet, and when she comes, you'll still be able to see your father. I'm sure she won't object. You yourself told me that she said she would look for him. She probably didn't want you to know that she was divorced, because she was afraid it might affect how people thought of you at the kibbutz. She wanted to be here first, and she never thought it would take so long. Have

144

you told anyone else about your visit with your father?"

"No. Not even Ruti."

"It's hard to keep all that bottled up inside you," said Hannah. "You can certainly tell people about your father and Lili."

"Suppose I'm asked if they're married?"

"Tell the truth."

"Suppose I'm asked if my parents are divorced?"

"They have to be if your father is remarried."

"My mother will be mad at me."

"No, she won't. She just didn't think the two of you would be separated for so long."

The bus appeared in the distance.

"Lydia," said Hannah quickly, "if you ask me, you can eat her cooking and go to hear her sing. You can visit them every other weekend, like all the boarding-school children on the kibbutz, and soon, when the summer vacation begins" — the bus pulled up and Hannah started up the steps while still talking — "you can even visit them every week. I'm sure they'll try to make things nice for you. It's your decision. See you soon!"

That talk set my mind to rest. I told Ruti everything and felt much better. And I wasn't worried anymore about what to say if her parents asked questions.

In the middle of the week my father surprised me by coming to the kibbutz. He arrived in the afternoon, when I was at the swimming pool. Our kibbutz had the only swimming pool in the whole area and we were very proud of it. Actually, it wasn't exactly a swimming pool. It was an irrigation pool with tarred, slanting sides, but it had benches and grass around it and even a lifeguard who locked up when he left. There was a hole in the fence for grownups who wanted a moonlight dip, but any child who tried sneaking in after hours was asking for trouble.

I liked being seen in the water by my father. He sat on the bench and I left my towel with him. I showed him how I swam and dived. After a while I was joined by some other children from my class and some older boys and girls. One of them was Shai, who was in charge of the nature corner and sometimes yelled at me when I did something wrong or forgot to turn off the water tap. He also laughed at me once when I was frightened by a rooster. Still, whenever we played "Here Come the Troops," he always chose me first for his team.

In case you don't know the rules, "Here Come the Troops" is a simple game. Two children stand on one side of the pool and shout, "Here come the troops!" The team on the other side has to jump into the pool and cross it without being tagged by the team in the water, and whoever is caught joins the water team until only the winner is left. Although I was one of the best swimmers in the whole school, I never managed to make it across against Shai. Even if I dived so deep that I touched the bottom and my ears hurt, he always caught me.

Once Ruti had said to me, "You let him catch you on purpose!"

At first I had been angry and said she was making it up. Afterwards I thought that maybe she was right. But she was just being jealous.

146

Dripping water, I went to sit by my father. He wrapped me in the towel.

"You're so tan and such a good swimmer! I wish Lili could see you now."

"You did love Mama once, didn't you?"

He sighed. "Every time I mention Lili, you talk about your mother. I don't want to discuss her now, Lydia. Some day when you're older I'll explain the whole thing to you."

"When is that?"

"I mean when you're a lot bigger. And by then maybe you'll understand by yourself."

I knew he'd say something like that.

"All right. But did you or didn't you?"

"I did."

"I have your wedding picture."

"You do? I'd like to see it."

"It's at Ruti's parents'. Did I tell you about them? They're my kibbutz family."

"I know. Shall we go?"

The two of us walked to my room. The dorm was deserted. We went to the shower and I dressed. Then we went to Ruti's parents'. When I opened the door without knocking, my father refused to step inside.

"Doesn't anyone lock doors around here?"

"Why should we?" I said proudly. "There are no thieves. Come on in."

"I'd rather not. I'll wait to be asked by Ruti's parents."

I brought the photograph outside. My father took a long look at it.

"Mama was very pretty," he said. "What is she like now?"

"She's still very pretty."

To tell the truth, she was prettier then. My father must have known that, though. He was handsomer in the photograph too.

"Would you like to see the horses?"

"You have riding horses?"

"Yes. I thought you knew."

On our way there he told me that he had been a good rider when he was young. "Maybe you got your love of horses from me," he said.

That was the sort of thing that my mother and grandmother, or even Ruti's parents, would say. Not just about the color of your eyes or how tall you were, but about everything, which always came from somebody or other. It was awfully annoying. Fine, so I resembled people in my family. Wasn't there anything about me that was just me?

"I got it from myself," I said.

My father laughed.

I told him that only sixth-graders and up could ride and take care of the horses, but that I could start riding lessons in the summer before sixth grade. Even now I sometimes came to watch the older children, and if they were short a hand they let me help out. My favorite horse was a big one called Farouk. The beginners were taught to ride on him, because he was very gentle. I also showed my father Meiska, who was much wilder. When Papa tried petting her muzzle, she tossed her head away. We watched the older children feeding the horses and one of them brushing down Farouk.

"Lydia," said my father, "I'd like you to come for the weekend."

I didn't answer right away. I thought for a minute. Then I said, "I don't know how to get to your house."

"This Friday I'll come to pick you up. After that you'll know how to come by yourself."

I agreed. I walked him to the road and waited with him at the bus stop. We sat without talking until the bus came.

"Papa, you come again, too!"

"I will," he said.

He kissed me and the bus drove off.

❊❊❊❊❊❊❊

On my second visit I ate whatever That Woman cooked. It was still a point of honor to say "thank you" and "please" in a syrupy voice, but I didn't always remember to do it. By the third or fourth visit I was talking to her pretty normally, and once I even accidentally called her by her name. That evening I had a bad conscience. *You're forgetting your mother, Lydia,* I told myself.

Sometimes on the kibbutz, too, I would remember my mother and be frightened because I didn't think of her more often. I felt terrible for her at such times.

My father didn't stroke Lili's cheek or put his hand on hers at the table anymore. Still, I couldn't help seeing how he looked at her and talked to her, even though I tried to ignore it.

149

The summer vacation came to an end. I was in the sixth grade now. I was happy to see Hannah again, and as soon as our first lesson was over I began telling her about That Woman.

"You should see how he looks at her and talks to her! It's awful. It's like . . . like I don't know what."

Hannah said, "Lydia, your father is in love with her and you're jealous."

I was furious. Who did she think she was? She was nothing but an English teacher! I may have told her all my secrets and she may have found my father for me — although it was really her husband who did it — but I was *not* jealous. Why should I be? My father was my father, it was as simple as that. Did she take me for Ruti? I didn't walk her to the bus for a whole week.

Whenever I came to visit, I could smell what Lili had cooked for me from outside the door. She also washed and ironed the clothes she and my father had bought me, which I wore only in the city. I had no choice but to go shopping with her. You couldn't expect my father to help me pick out clothes.

One time I brought two candles from the kibbutz and when they had gone to sleep that night and thought I had too, I tried Marioara's method for seeing my husband. Not that I believed in it — but as I stood with the burning candles in front of the mirror, my heart began to pound. No one appeared, but that night I dreamed that I saw a procession of people with long coats and hidden faces. Suddenly one left the others and walked toward me. I was about to see who he was when I was awakened by my own cry.

The door opened and my father came in. I could tell by the light in the window that it was almost day.

"Lydia, are you all right? You cried out in your sleep."

"I thought it was someone else," I said in a daze.

"What were you dreaming about?" He sat next to me on the bed.

"Just some dumb thing," I said.

All at once I told him about Marioara and the mirror, and we laughed at the memory of how frightened we both had been that time he surprised me in Bucharest.

"What happens if you have a bad dream or wake up crying in the dorm?"

"There's someone on night duty, but she's over by the nursery and can't hear us. Now and then she comes by to check up on us. Anyway, that's what we're told, but I hardly ever wake at night, and if I do, I just look at all my sleeping friends and go back to sleep myself. Ruti told me that when she was little she used to get up in the middle of the night and run back to her parents' room in her pajamas, even in the cold and the rain."

"Wasn't she scared?"

"I asked her that. She said it was scarier in the dorm."

"Why didn't she just sleep with her parents, then?"

"You can't do that on the kibbutz, Papa. Her father or mother brought her back to the dorm and sat with her until she fell asleep. One night she did it four times in a row, and they brought her back each time except the last."

"They finally gave in, eh?"

"No. It was morning by then. They went to work and left her in their room."

"Lydia, there's something I'd like to ask you. You don't have to give me an answer right now. You can think it over and we'll talk about it the next time. Would you like to come live with us?"

"But Papa, I'm waiting for Mama."

He kept on talking as if he hadn't heard me. He told me about the school that was near their house, and about the children I had once played with in the park, and about the room I would have to myself. He also promised that I could always return to the kibbutz if my mother came. That frightened me.

"Do you think that Mama might not come?"

"I'm sure she will, but it may take a long while. And besides, you can always spend part of your summer vacation there. The kibbutz takes city children for the summer months."

"Did you prepare a room for me because you thought I would come to live with you?"

"Yes. I didn't know that your mother was planning to settle in the kibbutz too."

"If I only come on weekends and holidays, will you still keep the room for me?"

"We'll always keep it for you. You needn't worry about that."

"I want to wait for Mama in the kibbutz," I said.

Every Saturday morning my father took me for a walk in the country and we picnicked just like the first time.

Lili stayed home. One weekend I stayed over until Sunday. Lili was singing at the soldiers' club that Saturday night and I wanted to hear her. I didn't mind that she sang beautifully. I even felt proud. She was at least as good as the actress with the red velvet dress and the spider brooch, even if she wasn't dressed as nicely.

I never let her put me to sleep, though. That was my way of staying loyal to my mother.

CHAPTER FOURTEEN

My Mother Arrives, But...

THE AUTUMN HOLIDAYS went by. Hanukkah arrived. The sixth-graders took part in a torchlight parade. It was a little scary, because the torches had big flames. You had to be careful to walk with your torch to one side to keep from burning the person in front of you. When we reached the dining hall, one of the older boys took each torch and plunged it into a barrel of water.

Once winter was over I began waiting impatiently for Passover. After it I would get to work with the horses. Also, the pool would be open.

When my father was found he had to start paying for me and I became a boarding-school child. To tell the truth, though, all my friends envied me, because now I had my own spending money. I also had two sets of parents, Ruti's and my father, and my own private room in the city, which stayed mine even though my father moved his desk back into it. He used the room as his study when I wasn't there, and his clothes hung in the closet beside mine.

I went to him every other weekend. On one of these visits I took my dolls and put them in the closet too. Sometimes I even played with them when no one was looking. So what if I was in the sixth grade? Even now I still like to play with dolls.

Lili always cooked some special treat. I told her how much I liked her cooking and how nicely she sang, and I even told my father how well she dressed. He asked me if I still liked her perfume, and we had a good laugh.

I didn't know how to feel about her. I honestly liked her and couldn't imagine my father without her, but I also wanted my parents to live together again. It wasn't very logical, but when I talked to Hannah she said that feelings often aren't.

Everything went on as usual until the day I received a telegram. Dina brought it from the office. My hands shook when I opened it. Although she knew what was in it, Dina didn't say a word. I read it at a glance, and then again word by word:

DEAR LYDIA I'LL SEE YOU SOON MUCH LOVE MAMA.

It came from Turkey. My mother would take a train from there as I had. I knew she couldn't possibly arrive that same day, or even the next one, but I couldn't stop myself from stealing off to wait that morning, afternoon, and evening for each of the bus's three arrivals. The next day I did it openly. By now all the children knew. Ruti started waiting for the evening bus with me, and each time it pulled up, my heart beat faster. No one getting off the bus was my mother, though.

That Friday I didn't know whether to go to my father's or not. Ruti's parents tried to convince me to go, but I couldn't. All I could think of was that my mother might come.

On Sunday morning my father phoned the office. "Lydia?"

"Papa?"

"Lydia, why didn't you come? We were expecting you. We were worried."

"Papa, I got a telegram from Mama."

"When?"

I told him.

I could hear the excitement in his voice when he said, "I've arranged for a certificate to be waiting for her at the British embassy in Istanbul. I hope she comes soon."

But another week went by with no sign of her, and when Friday came around again I decided to go to my father's. It was just my luck that my mother arrived that weekend! She came with a group of five immigrants. I was informed of it by Leah when I returned on the first bus Sunday morning and ran to my room to change clothes and get my schoolbooks. She was the last person I would have chosen to hear the news from.

"When?"

"Last night, when you were away."

The witch! But this was no time to talk back.

"Where are they?"

"In the shacks."

"What did you tell her?"

"That you went to visit your father and his wife."

"What did she say?"

"What do you mean, what did she say?"

"*What did she say?*" I shouted. "What's so hard to understand?"

"Oh, you mean *that*. She said, 'Lydia's found him? That's good.' "

"That's all?"

"She asked about you. I didn't tell her about the frog or the time you tore my dress."

"How about the time you dragged me into the boys' shower?" I called over my shoulder, already running toward the shacks.

"I didn't even tell her what gall you have!" she shouted back.

By now I was tearing along the path and not at all sure she could hear, but I yelled, "Leah, how many times do I have to tell you that it was a toad, not a frog?"

She yelled something too, but I was out of earshot.

The first shack was empty. The second had three rooms. The door to one of them was open, perhaps because of the heat, and two girls were fast asleep inside. The second door was shut so I knocked. The young man who opened it didn't speak Hebrew but was more than happy to talk in Romanian. I didn't have time for a conversation, though. All I wanted was to know where my mother was.

"What's her name?"

"Mrs. Hoffman."

He didn't know anyone by that name. "There's no Mrs. Hoffman in our group," he said.

"What do you mean, there isn't? I know there is! Ruth Hoffman, my mother!"

"You're right, there is a Ruth. I think they're in the last shack."

They? I knew there was a fifth person. I ran to the last shack. The first two rooms were empty and the third was locked. I knocked.

"Who is it?" my mother's voice asked in Hebrew.

"Mama, it's me!"

I heard all kinds of noises.

"One minute . . . just a minute."

It took her a long time to appear. I began to shift from foot to foot, the way I do when I'm made to wait. What was taking so long?

My mother opened the door in a nightgown, looking sleepy and disheveled. I flung my arms around her and we hugged hard. She pulled me back onto the bed with her. There was even an extra pillow there, waiting for me.

"There are such lovely people in the kibbutz," she said, wiping her tears. "I had a visit from the parents of your friend — what's her name — Ruti? They told me the nicest things about you."

Wait till she got to know Leah! And there were a few other pretty yucky types too. I didn't tell her that, though. She would find out for herself.

"But Mama, in what language did you talk to people?"

"In Yiddish. And if they didn't know any, in English. I spoke English to your friend's parents, too. And the kibbutz secretary is from Romania. Your housemother told me you were visiting your father. So you've found him!"

I studied her face. She didn't look angry at all.

"You know, Papa did send us certificates for Palestine. They just never reached us."

"I suppose we changed addresses a lot. When did he send them?"

"After he sent one to her. Because of Rommel. He waited for Rommel to be driven back."

"What made you decide to look for him?"

"Mama, you kept not coming and not coming!"

She let out a sigh. "My darling . . . " She began to cry.

"Did you know that they were married?"

"Really? No, I didn't."

"Why didn't you tell me that you were divorced?"

"What good would it have done for you to know?"

"I wouldn't have kept hoping that you would get back together and that he would leave Lili when you came. That's what!"

"I thought I would find him here and explain everything to you when we settled down. Did you tell everyone here that he's married?"

"Yes. They all know."

"Good. You've saved me a lot of explaining."

"But why didn't you tell me in Romania?"

"Because you have a big mouth and I didn't want all our friends and neighbors to know. Papa was gone anyway, so there was no need for it."

"Did Grandma know?"

"No."

"Who did?"

"No one."

"Were you ashamed of it?"

"That's none of your business. Yes, I was. What do you think? Any woman would be ashamed if her man left her for someone else, even if she didn't love him."

"And you didn't love Papa?"

"Actually, I did, but it's not like me to hold on to anyone against his will. How did you find him?"

I told her about Hannah and her husband.

"What can I say, Lydia?" You did exactly what you should have."

"I feel terrible that the day you happened to come . . . "

"Don't even think of it. It's not important. This room is such a mess! Tell me: how's Lili?"

"I guess she's all right," I said impassively.

"For my part, you can go on visiting them. Your father will always be your father, and you know that I'll always be your mother."

I didn't like the casual way she said it. How come she was being so generous? And my heart sank when she came out with that revolting remark about always being my parent that I was used to hearing from my father. I gave her a long look. She didn't seem the least bit unhappy.

"How come you stayed so long in Turkey? I went to the bus stop every day to wait for you."

"We wanted to do a bit of touring, Lydia. We were a group. Don't you have to go back to school?"

"Are you trying to get rid of me?" I rose indignantly from the bed. I couldn't understand what had happend to her.

"Lydia, how could you even think such a thing? It's just that . . . I have to explain something. No, don't go. I have something serious to talk to you about."

"Did something happen to Grandma?"

"Your grandmother is dead. She took a turn for the worse right after you left. She kept asking if I had heard from you, and when I told her that I had, she stopped worrying. She died in her sleep. I only hope I die as peacefully when I reach her age. She loved you very much."

I loved her too. Although my mother was still talking, I wasn't listening anymore, because I could see my grandmother's face in front of me and almost hear her laugh. My mother always said that I was like her. After a while, though, I began to pay attention again to what my mother was saying. And when I did, I almost ran from the room and slammed the door behind me.

"If that man ever comes here, I'm going to live with Papa!" I shouted.

"Calm down and stop screaming. I already told you when you were smaller never to call him 'that man.' His name is Lupo, and he's the best friend I have."

"I knew it! I knew it all along!"

161

"You knew we were married?"

"You're married?"

"We're married. We've come to Palestine together and we want to join the kibbutz."

I looked suspiciously around the room. That other pillow! And I had let myself put my head on it, even though the man who told me where my mother was had said "they" rather than "she"! To think that while *they* were gallivanting around Turkey, I was going to the bus stop day after day to wait for her!

"You're not Mrs. Hoffman anymore? Then what are you? Mrs. Lupo?"

"Lydia, sit down." She had noticed that I was staring at the pillow. "Sit on that chair. You can move the clothes. What are you staring at? All right, so they are his clothes."

"Where is he?"

Lupo crawled out from under the bed. He was wearing my father's pajamas, I swear, or at least a pair that looked exactly like them. And he was just like I remembered from the movie theater when we were friends, before the Iron Guard broke his leg and he met my mother. He made crawling out from under the bed look like something he was just pretending to do. I would have burst out laughing if I hadn't been so angry.

"Didn't I tell you — " he began, but my mother interrupted him.

"You keep out of this!" she said to him, and to me, "Say hello to Mister Lupo."

She was just as I remembered her, too. She had just arrived and she was already bossing everyone around. I was so used to being polite by now that I said "Hello" without even sounding sweet.

"Lydia," said Mister Lupo, and I could see that he meant it, "you've gotten so big and so pretty!"

I couldn't hate him. Not even for a little while. I simply stalked out of the room, without even slamming the door. My mother ran after me.

"Lydia," she called. "Lydia, come back!"

I didn't. I went to school and tried not to think about it. I sat through English class like a zombie. During recess Hannah called me over and we went outside.

"I heard that your mother is here. Is something wrong?"

I told her everything and started to cry. The only part I left out was about Lupo being under the bed.

"Let's go for a walk," she said.

We walked toward the nature corner. Hannah did the talking. This time too she talked in Hebrew. I don't remember exactly what she said, but she tried to explain that it wasn't so easy to be a parent, especially to be *my* father and mother, and especially in the middle of a war. She told me that parents had their own lives and weren't just fathers and mothers. As if I didn't know that already!

"Now you have one set of parents in the kibbutz and another in the city. You're rich!"

That didn't seem very funny to me.

"Go talk to your mother. She must be feeling terrible. Why, you haven't seen each other in months!"

It took that last sentence to make me realize that my mother really had come.

I ran back to her. By now, though, she was in a fighting

163

mood. She wouldn't even hug me until she saw that I was crying. Then we calmed down and had tea, and she said she had prepared a speech that I had to listen to. I listened. She said pretty much the same things that Hannah had, although not in the same words. She was angry and cross with me.

"I know that children can't see beyond the tips of their own noses. I was a child once, too. But you're not so little anymore, and it's time you understood! I'm willing to do a great deal for you, but not to ruin my own life."

I shrugged. She went on talking.

"I didn't count on our first meeting being like it was. I wanted to talk to you in private. To break it to you slowly. But we overslept and it didn't work out."

I had gotten accustomed to my father's "we's," and now I would have to get accustomed to my mother's, too.

"What do you have against Lupo? Didn't you like him when he was a pantomimist? Can't you think of him the way you did then? Forget about his leg being broken."

"I don't have anything against him, Mama. I'm a pretty old hand at all this."

"Are you referring to Lili?"

"Yes."

"Tell me, what is she really like?"

I could see that she was dying to know.

"You'll see for yourself a month from now."

"What does that mean?"

"Our school is putting on a show for the kibbutz's twentieth anniversary. We're rehearsing with a real director and I have a part. My teacher invited them."

164

"You see! You were so upset about losing your part in that play in Romania."

"I had the lead in it."

"Maybe you have a part for Lupo?"

At first that made me laugh. The parts were all given out. On second thought, though, why not add one for him? He wouldn't even have to know any Hebrew. I decided to talk to Giyora the director. His first reaction was like mine. "Impossible!" But his second reaction was like mine, too. "A pantomimist? I'd like to meet him."

My mother began working in the sewing shop, and Lupo was given a job in the barn. He was very proud of his new profession. Giyora gave him an audition, loved what he saw, and added a section to the prologue for him. At first I went to their shack after school every day, but I missed Ruti's parents and told my mother that I wanted to visit them, too. For the time being she agreed to Mondays and Thursdays, provided that afterwards it was she who walked me back to the dorm.

That Friday night I sat with my mother and Lupo at the Sabbath meal in the dining hall. Ruti's mother had told me that my mother "sewed divinely" and that Lupo was a "fantastic performer." I was beginning to feel proud of them.

On Saturday the three of us went for a walk in the fields. My mother and Lupo were in a gay mood and behaved like two teenagers, even though they were old people. I mean, they were at least thirty-five. Lupo practiced all kinds of jumps and threw sticks and stones, after which he tried getting me to play soccer with a ball he had made from some old sacks and a piece of rope he found. He told me that when he was a boy this was the only kind of ball he ever played with, because no one in his neighborhood could afford a real one.

"Where did you grow up?" I asked.

"In Dudeşti. Have you ever heard of it?"

"You bet I have."

I glanced at my mother, but she wasn't looking at me. She did agree to be the goalie, though. Suddenly she was like my memories of her from the time I was little.

They'll have another child too, I thought. It will be pretty embarrassing to have an old woman like my mother walking around the kibbutz with a big belly. Will it be a boy or a girl? I wanted them to have a girl, and my father and Lili to have a boy. My mother was a lousy goalie.

That afternoon they went with me to the pool. My mother sat on the grass and Lupo swam with me. He was a very good swimmer, even though he looked like a man who was just pretending to swim. He wore this funny bathing suit too. I wasn't sure if it was a real one or just some weird kind of underpants.

The weekend after that I went to my father's. Don't think he was happy to hear about Lupo. He was so annoyed that he began pacing up and down the room.

"What's the matter?" asked Lili.

"Nothing is the matter. It's just that she might have thought a little more about the . . . ."

He never finished his sentence, because it occurred to

him that *he* might have thought a little more about the child himself.

I decided that Lili was pretty smart. When I went to bed that night, she asked me, "Lydia, may I come with you and your father tomorrow?"

A week earlier I would have blown my top.

My father tucked me in and kissed me good night, then Lili bent down and kissed me, too, like him but without all the bristles.

Just because stepmothers and stepfathers are bad in fairy tales doesn't mean they really have to be like that, does it?

Before the two of them got up the next morning, I took out my dolls and sat them on my bed. It was time for one last ceremony.

"Are you my witnesses that I, Lydia Hoffman, do solemnly declare That Woman and That Man to no longer be my official enemies?" I asked in my most formal voice.

The dolls just sat there.

"We are your witnesses," I said for them.

Then we all shouted together, "Down with Fraulein Gertrud!"

I burst out laughing. My father and Lili were apt to think I was crazy, giggling to myself in my room!

I returned the dolls to their bag and got back into bed. I wasn't going to kiss Lupo. At least not before the wedding. I mean my own wedding. Because after the ceremony the bride always kisses all her friends and relatives, no matter how old they are. That's what I had seen on

the kibbutz. Which isn't any reason to jump to the con-
clusion that I plan to get married some day, because I
don't.

Not in real life, anyway.

You see, I have this new game that I play at my father's,
in which King Carol doesn't abdicate and leave Romania
with fifty railroad cars and his mistress after all. He stays
in his palace with his wife the Greek princess, and I marry
Prince Michael just as we had planned and the two of us
are King and Queen of Palestine. I wasn't about to pass
that up.

I'm not embarrassed to tell you that I go on playing
other old games of mine too, especially the one in which
Rommel catches Leah and shakes the living daylights out
of her. She's still my latest enemy for now.

A Last Word

I FIRST MET "Lydia" in a small army base overlooking the Sea of Galilee. (I put the name in quotes here because it isn't her real one.) I was nineteen years old and doing my army service, and she was the same age and doing hers. She was very, very tall and very, very thin. And pretty. And very funny. Funny on purpose, I mean. That was when I first heard some of her stories, like the ones about having her nannies fired in Bucharest. They stuck in my memory, and even more memorable was the portrait that they drew of a little girl who believed with all her heart that if only she wanted anything badly enough, whether it was being rid of That Woman or marrying a prince, she would find a way to get it.

Over the years, we continued to run into each other now and then. Lydia still lives on a kibbutz. She was an actress in the theater for a while, too, although not for very long, and she has also published a few books of poetry. In the end she married a rabbi. On the kibbutz she's in charge of the cooking, and she writes daily and weekly food columns in the newspapers. Besides good food, her favorite hobby is bridge. She still does whatever she feels like doing, and her close friends have to take her as she is today, too. She doesn't give them any choice.

Uri Orlev
Jerusalem 1993